———————————— ★ ————————————

A strong coppery odor wafted out to David as he silently studied the large stain on the new carpet that surrounded the dead man's head like a black halo. The stain pattern told David that death had not been immediate. The bullet had turned Jud into a vegetable instantly, but some part of his brain had survived a second or two, keeping the heart muscle pumping following the collapse to the floor. He asked his officers in a half whisper, "You guys keeping everybody out of here?"

"We've been trying," Melvin replied. "But trying to stop the Navajo was like trying to stop a windstorm."

Great, David thought angrily. Keeping this crime scene intact was about as simple as hitting the moon with a load of buckshot.

———————————— ★ ————————————

MURDER
on the
RED CLIFF REZ

MARDI OAKLEY MEDAWAR

TORONTO • NEW YORK • LONDON
AMSTERDAM • PARIS • SYDNEY • HAMBURG
STOCKHOLM • ATHENS • TOKYO • MILAN
MADRID • WARSAW • BUDAPEST • AUCKLAND

For Tom...my dearest friend

MURDER ON THE RED CLIFF REZ

A Worldwide Mystery/May 2004

First published by St. Martin's Press LLC.

ISBN 0-373-26493-3

Printed in U.S.A.

FOREWORD

THOUSANDS OF YEARS after Adam and Eve were
given the boot, the Ojibway, following the advice of
their prophet, went looking for the land where food
was said to grow on water. Their discovery of wild
rice in northern Wisconsin meant that Eden was re-
claimed. A few hundred years after this, the voya-
geurs —canoe-paddling Frenchmen—came on the
scene, looking for valuable pelts and native alliances
against the English. Behind them came the Black
Robes—the priests. The Ojibway subsequently became known as the Chippewa and were dutifully
baptized and given French names.

A little more than six years later, Eden underwent
a severe transformation as well as its own name
change, to Wisconsin. Paul Bunyan and his ilk discovered the bounty of the North Woods, primarily
the ancient white pines growing four hundred feet
tall and with trunk bases as wide as Chevys. In an
ax-swinging frenzy, Paul and the boys reduced most
of Wisconsin to a stumpy prairie, with the exception
of pockets of a few hundred acres.

During the subsequent years while the United States learned to become a country, then a world power, the North Woods made a comeback. The new growth was not spectacular, but the newly emerging forests were enough to serve as a subtle reminder of what once had been. Under wiser management the few surviving pockets of old growth became protected as a national treasure, and with the abundance of wildlife, Wisconsin became known as the sportsman's paradise. The best-kept secret of these modern times is that the capital of this nirvana is not Madison, Green Bay, or Milwaukee. It is, for those in the know, the picture-postcard-perfect New Englandesque town nestled serenely on the banks of Lake Superior.

They call it Bayfield.

Just up from the town of Bayfield, and situated on the tip of the peninsula, surrounded by the Apostles Islands, is the Chippewa Reservation of Red Cliff. Bayfield and Red Cliff are good neighbors, and since the days the Wisconsin legislature declared state supremacy, the Bayfield County sheriff's office and the tiny Red Cliff police department have enjoyed a friendly competitiveness, and for the most part have been mutually cooperative. But this friendliness has never been tested because speeding, drunk and disorderly, and the occasional domestic and/or bar fight are about as wild as the off-season in the deep woods has ever been known to be. Red

Cliff doesn't have a jail, so a serious offender—a fist-swinging drunk—can look forward to a lockdown in the Bayfield County jail until his appearance before the judge in the tribal courthouse in Red Cliff. Sentencing runs the gamut: a severe lecture, a hefty fine, or in worst cases, both.

A few years back Red Cliff had an abundance of indigenous felons known as one-month lifers. It used to go this way: When a man's family was hungry, he'd take a deer; then the game wardens would take him to the Bayfield County lockup. The fella would serve his time, get out, take another deer, go on another month vacation. Life continued in this peculiar circular pattern until once again the Chippewa tribes decided, *Well, hey! This is ridiculous.* That bit of tribal wisdom, coupled with clear treaty language and a rather lengthy court struggle, resulted in Indian hunting lands and seasons being duly extended. Able to hunt in ceded territories, Chippewas were no longer being locked up and fed at Bayfield County's expense. Life in and around Lake Superior's most northern region subsequently became a little dull. Especially after the October Apple Fest, when the last of the camera-toting tourists faded and the populations of Bayfield and Red Cliff settled down to about two thousand. It became duller still when the lake effect storms howled and the temperatures struggled to soar above minus twenty. During the winter the number of rez cops falls from five to three: a dispatcher to answer the phone; two to drive around displaying a presence.

There hasn't been a deliberate murder in this woodland paradise in anyone under fifty's living memory.

ONE

Tuesday, May 4, 1999, 7 a.m.

IRENE GIRARD LIKED to walk her dog. It was a stupid dog, as big and as ugly as an inescapable nightmare, but it loved her to pieces and she loved it right back, so she walked it on a chain leash mornings and late afternoons without fail, come peaceful sunrise or raging blizzard. Irene and her dog were walking down the center of the dirt track that passed the fancy new house belonging to the tribal attorney when she heard and saw something terribly disturbing. She went right home and told her husband Ned, who lost no time clambering inside his rattling truck and speeding off to Buffalo Bay Store. He'd told his wife they needed milk. The Girards didn't take milk, not even in their spoon-dissolving coffee. Ned had been in the store almost an hour talking to a group of men when Benny Peliquin, who did buy milk, came in. With Benny's appearance, Ned began re-telling Irene's story all over again, the early morning crowd of regulars still quietly attentive. Well, why not? Ned's story was far more interesting than the current news that Ricky Dehue was moving his trailer house.

"Irene's dog, you know, Brutus, eh?" Ned pulled a face. "I hate that dog. It shits everywhere. Puts out turds as big as an elephant's." Ned's face cleared. "Anyhow, Irene was a'walking Brutus and they was going on down the road so's Brutus could leave elephant turds on other folks' yards when she hears a big ruckus comin' outta your cousin's new house."

From all outward appearances, Benny Peliquin, a tall reedy man with a weathered face who spoke in Lake Superior commercial fisherman's mumble, was only mildly interested. Benny's expression was impassive as he counted the change lying in the callused palm of his hand. He felt Myra Chigog intently watching him as she leaned across the countertop, resting the upper part of her body on folded arms. The milk Benny was in the process of buying stood near her arms, condensation trickling down the plastic container, creating puddles on the counter's Formica. He also felt the steady gaze of the half-dozen men forming a semicircle around him as they sipped their coffee from white foam cups.

"That was a dollar twenty-five, you said, eh?"

"Twenty-six," Myra corrected.

Benny placed the exact change on the counter, picked up the drippy container by its side handle.

Turning, he bumped chests with Ned Girard. The older man was determined to say what he obviously felt Benny needed to hear.

But as Ned was champing at the bit to tell tales about Benny's family members, Benny issued a warning. "Ned, I'm figuring you're just about to step where you don't belong. That's dangerous ground, chum."

Ned Girard audibly gulped. Benny was getting him all wrong. Sure, everybody knew...but that wasn't what he was getting at. No, sir, that wasn't what he was meaning at all. To smooth over a rough moment, Ned spilled the beans.

"Like I was tryin' to tell you. My Irene came home sayin' she'd heard screaming over at your cousin's. She said she was just standing in the road wonderin' what in the world, when she seen them two little kids come runnin' outta the side of that house. They went straight for the trees. She couldn't see no path or nothing, but she said them kids looked to her like they knew just where they were a-goin' because once they hit the woods, they just disappeared. Then the yellin' started up again. This time it was so bad that it scared Brutus an' that damn dog took off, pullin' Irene right off her legs. Once that dog gets to runnin', the fool don't know when to quit. Hell, Irene was flappin' like a flag behind him when Brutus came gallopin' into our yard."

Ned crossed his arms over his chest, his expression grave. "Now, Benny, I know I don't have to tell you that this ain't the first time yellin' has been heard comin' outta that house."

Complete silence descended, Buffalo Bay Store's early morning audience holding its collective breath. Ned and Benny continued to stare at each other. They held the stare for so long that the morning regulars were on the verge of keeling over from lack of oxygen. Still not saying a word, Benny finally turned on his heel, taking himself and the container of milk out of the store. Through the glass doors the crowd gawked as Benny ambled toward his truck and climbed in. Seconds later the truck roared out of the parking lot.

Ned Girard offered another opinion. "Fellas, purty quick a few things around here are gonna get real bad."

Behind him the Chippewa version of a Greek chorus promptly sounded: "Enh-enh!"

Tuesday, May 4, 8 p.m.

IN ASHLAND, a forty-minute drive from the rez, and inside the BIA's Great Lakes Agency located on the second floor of the Ashland Post Office, C. Clarence Begay paced, gnawing the knuckle of his right hand, his mind working as furiously as his teeth. C. Clarence had been with the bureau for twenty years. He was Irish-Navajo, very proud of the Irish bit, even though other than a pug nose poised incongruously on a wide, heavy face, the man displayed no trace of his Celtic ancestry. A short-limbed, thickset man (the thickness due to an almost religious commitment to green chili and hot buttered corn tortillas), C. Clarence was consistently thought to be a decade above his actual forty-three years.

C. Clarence hated Wisconsin. In his opinion, the northernmost state was equivalent to hell on earth. For one thing, the Chippewas had an overabundance of French blood oozing through their veins. For another, they talked too fast and sounded Canadian: for example, everything they said habitually ended with *eh.* They also called everybody *chum.* C. Clarence did not like being called *chum.* It made him feel like something about to be fed to sharks. During his first foray into the Lanes, the Red Cliff watering hole, the *chums* and *ehs* were flying so thick and fast that he hadn't been able to enjoy a simple beer.

Wisconsin had too many trees, tall suckers growing just too damn close together for someone who had been raised in an endless desert, a land so unobstructed that tomorrow was a visible haze on the horizon. In Wisconsin, C. Clarence couldn't see squat because there was always a jackass tree in the way. And he was secretly terrified of becoming hopelessly lost inside all that greenery. After a year, most of it spent suffering through the most appalling winter of his life, C. Clarence realized that he was a raging claustrophobic.

But he wasn't thinking about any of that as he paced and mindlessly chewed his knuckle. He was thinking of the way he'd been used, duped, pulled into something that filled him with absolute panic. He wasn't a criminal. He was simply a sucker. But no judge on earth would ever believe him. And the Chippewas...

His hands covering his face, C. Clarence groaned. He indulged his fear for a moment before steadying his resolve. Then, with effort, he forced his hands away, lifting his chin in a determined fashion. He had to do something to save himself. He knew he would never make it through a stint in Leavenworth.

Tuesday, May 4, 10:30 p.m.

"DADDY!" IMOGEN whisper-screamed into the telephone. It's one thing to be hysterical with fear, quite another to wake the kids with it.

"Jeanie?" the sleepy male voice croaked in response. She heard a tiny squeaking sound and realized her father was forcing his eyes open. A little more awake now, her father yawned and asked, "What's the matter, baby?"

Imogen said hurriedly, "I have to come home, Daddy." A trembling hand swiped tears from the exquisite face that once belonged to Miss Cherokee

Nation Princess, 1989. For the last decade an edgy woman with a nervous smile and hollow laugh had been posing as the former beauty queen. The doppelganger even had the nerve to wear Imogen's clothing as it frivolously signed her name to credit card receipts. Both entities called themselves Imogen Boiseneau.

A great long distance away, in the town of Tahlequah, Oklahoma, Imogen's father had come wide awake. Her saying that she needed to come home had even propelled him out of bed. His wife, Brenda, Imogen's mother, switched on the bedside light, watching bleary-eyed as her husband paced, stretching the telephone cord as far as it would go while he ran a hand through his steel-gray buzz cut. Brenda sat up, stuffing pillows between her back and the bed's headboard. By the time she finished this simple task, her husband had turned and was pacing back toward her end of the bed.

Retired Chief Justice of the Cherokee Nation Warren Otis was a devoted parent. Imogen was his only child. His ability to protect his daughter ended the day he'd handed her over in marriage to Judah Boiseneau. Since that day, Justice Otis blamed himself for his daughter's descent into marital hell. For over ten years he'd choked on the guilt.

"I want you to listen to—"

He was cut off by his daughter's earsplitting shriek. A second later his daughter spoke hurriedly into the phone, and what she was saying hit him with such a brutal force, his face drained. Brenda Otis noticed that her husband now stood rooted to the floor, his ruddy coloring becoming chalky. The man known for being unflappable under any circumstances (and in Cherokee politics this was the stuff of legend) now looked white as a corpse. Terror seizing her, Brenda clutched the front of her nightdress. She screamed, ''For God's sake, what's wrong?''

Warren Otis raised his eyes, and for a second or two looked at his wife of over thirty years as if he didn't know her. Then his color came back in a rush. Impatiently he waved Brenda into silence as he listened to their daughter. Then Warren Otis commenced to yell.

''Jeanie, get the hell out of that house. Don't bother to pack. Put the kids in the car and drive to Duluth. By the time you get to the airport, tickets will be waiting. Do you understand?''

Imogen, the real Imogen, as the alter ego she'd relied on for years had suddenly done a bunk, sat folded in a wing chair, forehead resting on her knees. ''Daddy—''

Warren Otis bellowed, ''I asked, Do you understand?'' Without waiting for Imogen's response, he slammed the phone down and grabbed the telephone book off the nightstand's lower shelf, almost ripping each page apart in his hurried search for Northwest's 1-800 number.

"Yes," Imogen whispered to no one. She tried to cradle the receiver. Trouble was, she couldn't make her hand let go. Looking down at the back of her hand, she saw that her knuckles were shining through the skin like a row of tiny white skulls. As quickly as the thought formed, a spasm wracked her entire body.

Wednesday, May 5, 4:15 a.m.

LITTLE SAND BAY on the Red Cliff Reservation jutts out into Lake Superior. Deep in the woods, about a half mile back from Lake Superior, heavy rains beat against a solitary log cabin, wind rattling the surrounding tree limbs. Amid this noise, Tracker, like a drowning victim, came violently awake: upper body arched, mouth opened, face aimed toward the rafters as she sucked in a load of air. The storm had nothing to do with her blast into wakefulness. Or with the fact that she was shaking as hard as the leaves on the wind-lashed trees. This was purely the effect of the dream that still held her in its relentless grip as she sat in the bed, legs bent, heart hammering inside her chest.

It took time and concentration to obliterate the face she had seen in her dream. Finally it faded, then was gone. Able to breathe a bit more easily, she slowly curled backward until she was again resting against the pillows. Lying very still, eyes straining against the darkness, she listened to the winds howl and the rain tick against the bedroom windows.

And then Cher commenced to sing inside her skull. "Do you believe in love after love?" Cher's song got caught in a merciless loop (echo effect included). In order to break free of it, Tracker yelled, "Hell no!" at the ceiling.

Startled awake by his mistress, Animush (Dog) stirred on the pallet at the foot of the bed, then yawned a loud doggy yawn. Animush—Mushy, for short—rose; toenails clicking against the floor, the huge brown cur moved toward the side of the bed. Mushy was used to his mistress's nocturnal misery. This had been happening night after night for about six months now, and Mushy had learned just what to do to rouse his mistress. Nudging a wide cold nose against her even colder hand, the big dog flipped that hand until it partially settled on the broad space just above two concerned dark eyes. After a minute or so, that seemingly lifeless hand began to stroke Mushy's rough fur. This was a good sign. A minute more of petting, and the woman he knew and slavishly loved spoke in a near-normal tone.

"Hey? Who's up for coffee?"

Mushy barked as Tracker threw back the heavy quilts. On a nice day the cabin's lone human occupant enjoyed a view of Sand Island. This morning the view was obliterated by cloud cover. The light inside the cabin's workroom came by way of overhead fluorescent tubes running the length of the ceiling in a utilitarian-stark room of unfinished sheet rock covering insulation that covered log walls. The bluish lights reflected off rough plank floorboards liberally splattered with layers of rock-hard clay blobs. In the far left corner a Franklin wood-burning stove set up off the floor on a pallet of bricks did its best to quash the morning chill. Even though it was technically spring, May in Wisconsin was more often than not monkey-butt-ugly cold.

The first thing Karen Charboneau—known to family and friends as Tracker—did after climbing out of bed was feed splits to the living room stove and then the workroom stove. Within minutes both stoves were glowing cherry red but the cabin remained cold, which was why Tracker hadn't bothered to change out of the long johns and thick socks she'd slept in. Standing at the work counter, coffee mug in hand, she thoughtfully studied the greenware firing schedule while the toe of her right foot scratched at the ankle of her left leg. The workroom radio, tuned to FM 88.9, emitted Muddy Waters's throaty warbling. A rez station, WOJB did its best to hit every level of musical taste. Absolute bite-ya-in-the-ass blues was aired only during the wee hours.

Tracker's favorite time and music.

In the corner behind her was a mammoth foot-powered potter's wheel. Two of the room's walls were covered with floor-to-ceiling shelves, each shelf crowded with green pots of various sizes. Hence the need for a firing schedule. Tracker's studio was the largest and most used section of the cabin. In truth, Tracker was so focused on the needs of her studio that she'd had to be goaded by her father into making the remainder of the cabin habitable.

She was the only girl in a family of men, and at age six she'd realized that her best weapon, a technique guaranteed to drive her father and brothers nuts, was to be stubborn. She was twenty-five now, stood five feet five and weighed one hundred and nine pounds, five of those pounds from her waist-length hair. Every inch and pound of her was stubborn. For months she'd been stubborn about her cabin. But this time George Charboneau lost patience with his daughter. After the spring walleye spearing season, George marshaled his four sons, and over Tracker's protests interior walls went up, making the bathroom and bedroom areas private. The remainder of the cabin, the living room and kitchen, were left open. A door off the kitchen led into the workroom. George and sons went on to wall off a section of the workroom, creating a tiny mudroom with its own step-up porch. The mudroom was little more than a windowless cell with a bare light-bulb and a bench. Not only did the new addition keep excess snow and mud from being tromped in, it stopped precious heat from being sucked out whenever Tracker opened the door.

The front door, at the center of the cabin's front wall and sheltered by a covered porch, was used only by visitors. The bedroom and bathroom were heated by freestanding electric heaters and the kitchen stove ran off propane. With the advent of the mudroom, those splits were stacked against the little porch and covered with a tarp to keep the wood dry. There wasn't anything on the front porch now but a pair of rustic hand-hewn rocking chairs. As of last spring, the cabin had its own well and septic system. Fifty feet behind the cabin, there was yet another tarp covering firewood, and close to that a kiln, which looked for all the world like a huge Hopi bread oven. Tracker used the kiln from the late spring until the first frost. Long winters were spent working the potter's wheel or sculpting at the work counter.

Right after she finished her studies at the Min-neapolis Art Institute her father began nagging her to come home. George Charboneau didn't want his only daughter living in a big city all on her own. He'd stayed on the subject for weeks, calling her at all hours of the day and night. Still, for reasons of her own, Tracker hesitated. Then the matter was taken out of her hands when her landlord raised her rent out of her range. Still stubborn about returning to Red Cliff, she began looking for another apartment. The best places she could find at the price she could pay weren't half as comfortable as the apartment she was being forced to leave, and the neighborhoods felt risky. The deciding factor came when she sat down with a pencil and paper and did the math. Any way she figured it, living back on the rez cut her expenses by more than half.

Financially defeated, Tracker went home.

The first few months of being home in Red Cliff were right up there with living in a fishbowl, she being the queen guppy. Too many people knew far too much about her life, which was discussed in full detail in the three gossip meccas: Buffalo Bay Store, Peterson's Groceries, and (God save us) the Lanes. The last was so called because it had begun life as a bowling alley, then evolved into a bar/pool hall/restaurant attached to the Isle Vista Casino. The evolution had everything to do with the fact that the *waiabishkiwedjig* (white tourists), eager to pour quarters into the casino slots, felt nonplussed about doing that when just next door—literally, as there is only a doorway between the casino and the Lanes—beer-drinking Shinabes could be seen walking around, every last man jack armed with a bowling ball. While such a scene was hardly Custer's last view, nervousness being what it is and the lifeblood of the casino threatened, the Council voted and the Lanes was forever changed from a bowling alley into a bar/pool hall/restaurant.

What the Council could not do, nor indeed any power on earth, was do away with the infamous Mug Row, the stretch of bar under the overhang that sported privately owned beer mugs. Mug Row has always been, will always be, the official side of the bar for the commercial fishermen from around three p.m. until last call, making Mug Row the source for gossip and even for one or two insurrections. The last uprising, about a month prior to Tracker's return, concerned a dummy Chippewa placed on a bench to advertise an antique shop in the suburb of Superior known as Alleouz.

Oooh, Mug Row really went into a flap over that one, the bar talk coming thick and hard, clearer heads coming up with the plan to picket the shop while carrying placards reading FREE THE FAUX SKIN. But by then Tracker had come home, and as watching her trying to ignore the fact that David Lameraux still lived and breathed was even more interesting, the dummy was forgotten.

While Tracker's life may have kept Mug Row amused, for her it was becoming so intolerable that the cabin her father and brothers were building for her on her land assignment was nothing more than walls and plastic sheeting over the windows when she moved in bags and potter's wheel. She hadn't cared that she'd have to wait for electricity, a well, and a septic tank. All she cared about was that the cabin was hidden away from the public eye. Ah, baby, that was bliss. But bliss invariably dissipated whenever she had to venture back into the mainstream.

On days like today.

"Damn!" She slammed the coffee mug down, tepid coffee sloshing onto the counter. Tracker didn't notice. She was too busy battling her fears of seeing David as she pulled a packing container out from beneath the workbench. Mushy, stretched snoozing on the floor, raised his shaggy head. The dog watched her with the same big brown eyes that had once gazed so forlornly from the half-starved puppy sitting shivering by the side of the road. Tracker had stopped the truck, got out, and called the poor little thing to her. Hesitantly it came, sides all caved in from hunger, thick coat matted with mud and jumping with fleas. She took the puppy home, fed it, and bathed it. The puppy who had once fit neatly inside her hands had grown up to be as big as a deer. He was also one smart dog—clever enough to recognize a Town Day. He knew to submit to the occasion with a whipped-dog whine and a submissive thumping of meaty tail against the floor.

Looking back over her shoulder Tracker frowned in irritation, her brows forming a V at the bridge of her nose. For some unknown reason, something else to annoy the breath out of her, Mushy was in full wretch mode. "What the hell's the matter with you?"

Mushy's tail immediately stopped. As his mistress stomped away, crescent rings of white showed beneath the sad eyes that followed her. Oh, this was a Town Day, all right. And until Town Day was over, there was precious little Mushy could do but flatten out on the floor and hang on like a stubborn drunk.

THE CHICKEN COOP, a neighborhood in Red Cliff, earned its nickname after every house in the subdivision was churned out as a two-story cube with a clerestory. The repeated design was the brainchild of an architect hired by the HUD housing people. The architect had been young and cursed with the taste of paste—and not the good kind kindergartners love to eat by the handful. In one of the houses on Bear Paw Lane, David Lameraux, half asleep, rolled toward the bedside table, his hand flailing about until it located the small alarm clock. A final slap put an end to the offensive buzzing. Prying one eye open, he read the time: 6 a.m.

David had been living in the house for two years. He'd gotten it back in the good ole days when he'd thought he was going to be married. The engagement ended the day his beloved had gotten all hot about something, and when he asked her what was wrong, she'd said the most loathsome thing a woman can ever say to a man: "You know exactly what you did!"

No, he didn't. He hadn't then (which is why he'd asked), and he certainly didn't now. Unwrapping himself from the tangle of sheets and electric blanket, David Lameraux staggered out of the bedroom, which other than the bed was furnished with cardboard boxes and a sheet covering the window. He clumped down the bare wood stairs and through the living room, which was decorated in Early Male: a big-screen TV, the latest sound system, wall-to-wall beige carpeting with wide brown footpaths, a Salvation Army couch, three deck chairs, an unfinished-plank-and-cinder-block bookshelf crammed with paperbacks (Elmer Kelton westerns and Stephen King thrillers), and more sheets posing as curtains on the windows.

Taking the brown pathway that cut a left through an open portal, David arrived in the kitchen. Yawning, he turned on the overhead light only to quickly blink against the sudden brightness. The sky outside the window over the sink was still as black as midnight and the rain hopping against the windowpane sent a chill that raised goose bumps all over his lean body, all six foot two inches of it. In an effort to bring a little warmth into his immediate world, he turned on the electric oven, rolling the temperature setting to 500 degrees. Next, he poured gummy sludge out of the Mr. Coffee pot into the sink, and from the swing basket he threw away some nasty-looking old grounds. The subsequent task involved rinsing and filling the pot with tap water and putting a new paper filter in the basket. He was scooping Maxwell House French Roast into the newly pre-pared basket when he began to smell something funny.

Not funny ha-ha. Funny God-awful.

His eyes flashed wide as he remembered (too late) that he'd stashed an extra large pizza in the oven, what? Three, four days ago? He dropped the coffee scoop, dry grounds creating more chaos on the al-ready cluttered counter, and dashed for the oven. Opening the oven door was a big mistake. Huge. The stink of baking cardboard and old pizza per-vaded every corner of the small kitchen before he had time to slam the door again.

David was someone meant to be married because on his own, the boy was pitiful. His whole trouble was, the woman he wanted to be married to wouldn't even speak to him except during the three times she'd had to work for him, helping locate idiot tourist deer hunters who'd gotten themselves lost. She'd had to talk to him then, oh yes indeedy, be-cause he was the chief of the rez police. As a tracker paid by the Council, she'd had to take orders directly from him. David could be a malicious little sod when he wanted to be, and to get back at her for that "You know exactly what you did!" he'd been as insufferable as he could possibly be. But did any of this petty revenge heal his wounded pride?

Nope.

TWO

THELMA FRENCHETTE WAS distraught. Always the first to arrive at work, Thelma, a woman in her fifties, took mothering her coworkers very seriously. Especially the young women, who if they weren't watched were likely to slack off. Young women today, eh? But just at the moment, thoughts of lackadaisical twenty-somethings had been zapped right out of her mind. In fact, lucid thoughts of any stripe were impossible. Because Thelma was in such a daze, her balance wasn't what it should be, and she braced her hands against the corridor walls as she slowly made her way down the hallway bisecting the warren of offices.

"My God," she breathed, repeating the words like a mantra as she moved unsteadily onward. "My God, my God, my God." She finally arrived in the reception area, a triangular zone central to the building. Stumbling now because she no longer had walls for support, she barely made it to the desk, which was situated behind a glass barrier. She looked like a relieved rummy as she collapsed in the desk chair. She sat there for a full minute, glazed eyes staring beyond the portraits of past Tribal Chairmans displayed on the paneled wall facing the reception desk. For several minutes her mind refused to budge beyond the thought *He can't be dead.*

But he was. No human being, not even Judah Boiseneau, could lose that much blood—and all over the brand-new carpeting!—and still be alive. The office coffeemaker, directly behind her on the shelf above the built-in filing cabinets, began to gurgle, the boiling water emptying from the maker's cistern into the glass decanter. The hiss of the steam and the gurgle were ordinary noises that at any other time Thelma would have heard without noticing. In this situation the sounds were enough to send her jerking straight up in the swivel chair. After the violent start she knew she could no longer endure being all alone in the empty building with a *tchibai,* a dead person.

Thelma snatched up the receiver, then punched nine for an outside line. She watched her fingers dial the first phone number that came to mind. Thelma had been a widow for ten years, shunning any thoughts of ever remarrying—mainly because she reveled in being a Frenchette, a certified member of Red Cliff's most predominant family. People in trouble always called family first, right? Yes, definitely. And as Thelma was definitely in trouble, she turned to the family member able to do her the most good.

The instant she heard his voice a smidgen of the fog inside her brain lifted. But not enough. Thelma Frenchette, big-deal career woman, was coming off like a nine year-old whimpering to Daddy about bullies on the playground. Seconds later her brother-in-law shouted, "For God's sake, Thelma, call the cops! I'll be there as soon as I can get my damn pants on."

Thelma pushed the button for another extension, cutting her brother-in-law off, and dialed nine yet again, then the number for the police. After four rings, Elliott Raven, the police dispatcher and lone body in the cop shop, picked up. Words tumbled out of Thelma.

"Elliott? Perry told me to call because, I, you know, get in first and I was doing, you know, what I always do, checking around, making sure everything was okay while I waited for the coffee. But I found…"

Thelma's mind went blank. Her lips continued to move, and vaguely, she heard her own voice. She could only trust that the sounds she made were intelligible to Elliott's attentive ear. Actually, the police station was only across the way. Instead of using the phone, all she really had to do was stick her head out the front door and yell. But yelling wasn't professional. Her brother-in-law was a very professional person. He used to be in marketing for IBM. Now he was the Tribal Chairman. Thelma basked in Perry's reflected glory and patterned her demeanor after his remote, businesslike manner.

"Thel?" Elliott Raven yelled in her ear.

Thelma snapped back into the moment. Realizing that she probably hadn't spoken for a while, she opened her mouth, but more words refused to come.

"Thel?"

Thelma Frenchette began to sob.

AFTER RECEIVING THE CALL, Elliott Raven, tall, lanky, and hovering somewhere in his sixties, found himself too busy to dwell on incidentals. The percolator stood idle as he radioed two patrol officers, managing to catch them just before they went for breakfast. Then he telephoned David's house and got no answer. Elliott then tried raising David on the com line.

David wasn't in the patrol car. As Elliott's voice squeaked through the radio receiver, David was standing inside Buffalo Bay Store, Styrofoam cup of coffee in hand, laughing and slapping with three morning regulars, all of them having a go at the store's owner about the iffy condition of the Baked Fresh bear claws.

"Well, of course they was baked fresh," Ned Girard was saying. "What the hell kind of fool bakes stale?"

"If youse boys don't like my sign, youse can go screw yourselves."

"Don't go all cranky." David laughed. "We're not worried about how they were baked. We'd just like to know how long they've been sitting since then."

"Well, that I forget," the owner conceded. "Besides, I only make pastry signs. You want a goodies calendar, call Hugh Hefner. Now, you want a bear claw or not?"

"Yeah," David said, rooting in his faded jeans pocket for additional change. Because he hadn't been to the Laundromat in a week, he was reduced to his last cop shirt. The shirt was tucked into fairly clean jeans. Because he was wearing jeans, he of course had on cowboy boots. On his head was his favorite baseball cap, emblazoned with the insignia of the Duluth Superior Dukes. A hard-core fan of the minor league, David wore the cap with *every-thing*. Even the black suit he'd worn to his cousin's funeral, at which he'd been a pallbearer. "Scrape off some of that fuzzy green stuff and give me one."

"But, Davey," Ned Girard joked, "the green fuzz is the best part."

"You ought to know," another regular hooted. "You've had two."

DAVID WAS FEELING a bit better about the morning as he climbed into the car. That emotion bit the dust when he finally heard his dispatcher.

"David? You even got your radio on?"

Lifting the handset from the dashboard console, David keyed the mike. "I have now."

"Where the hell are you? I've been callin' an' callin'."

"Don't nag, Elliott," David said. As he waited to pull out of the parking lot, two school buses went by on Highway 13, followed by five cars heading for the town of Bayfield. "I stopped in at Buffalo for coffee and now I'm waiting out the rush-minute traffic."

Elliott went a tad nuts.

David keyed the mike again. "Elliott, if this is official, take a deep breath and do the numbers."

Able to pull out now and going in the opposite direction of the former traffic, he listened as Elliott loudly paged through the lists of codes. Even though Elliott Raven had been a dispatcher for over two years, he still couldn't remember the call numbers. The dispatcher's pluses were that he'd never called in sick, was willing to work overtime without pay, and was the only human able to manage the department's old-fashioned percolator. David pressed his booted foot against the accelerator, and his patrol car picked up speed as it traveled along Blueberry Road. Elliott cursed as he fruitlessly searched the codebook. David knew then that even though the storm had lessened and the sun was poking holes in the lowering clouds, the warming spring day would not be properly appreciated. Something had his dispatcher all aflutter. And whatever was fluttering the normally laid-back Elliott had to be a pure-o-tee doozy.

Ever calm, David keyed the radio mike. "Am I gonna find some coffee when I get there?"

Elliott blurted out a rush of Ojibway.

David keyed the mike again. "English, Elliott. You know the Bayfield County boys are listening. You're only suppose to speak English when you're on the air."

Elliott Raven informed David in Ojibway that the Bayfield County deputies were all the sons of low-down stinky skunks.

Chuckling, David replied evenly, "Yeah, but your sister loves 'em."

The dispatcher squawked irately. Over Elliott's noise, David asked a sensitive question. "Have you sent a car to the...incident?"

"*Niji* (Two)."

David winced. Two units meant something big. Before Elliott could tell both him and the Bayfield County sheriff's department just what that something was, David threw away his own rule about speaking only English over the airwaves.

Elliott quickly countered with *"Nin nissitawen-dan*. My lips is zipped. Over an' out, an' ten-four."

A pained expression stealing over his handsome face, David replaced the mike.

THREE GAME WARDENS were standing in the parking lot that fronted the plain single-storied station shared by the police department and the tribal game wardens. The rez cops and the wardens were not happy office-mates. The wardens' main complaint was that the cops habitually parked anywhere they wanted to, only rarely in designated areas. The game wardens were fussy guys. Just for spite David rolled between the white lines, came to a stop in the slot marked CHIEF WARDEN, and shut off the engine. The furious wardens were on him the second he climbed out of the car. He was head and shoulders taller than any of them, but this was one morning when his superior height failed to intimidate.

"What are you doing here?" one of them asked, his tone incredulous. "Ain't you supposed to be over at the Tribal Courthouse?"

With practiced calm, David checked his wristwatch, a Christmas gift from one of his nephews. Peter Pan's stubbier arm was pointing to the eight while the longer one was pointing at the two. Eight-ten.

The Moccasin Telegraph was scary. If the game wardens already knew the strictly official police business, they'd likely already spread said strictly official business. Then too there was the problem of privately owned scanners. Every family on the rez owned one. They might not be able to afford TV, but man, they had a scanner. It had to be a nosy Indian thing. David didn't know any white people who even wanted a scanner. Adjusting the baseball cap on his head, David ambled by the game wardens, felt three pairs of eyes glaring at him. He refused to appear rushed, keeping his long-legged stride even.

Elliott met him at the door, pulling it open with such force that David found himself being hurtled inside. The first sight visitors saw was the battered wooden reception counter, where the public met the police. Behind the counter was an open squad room furnished with five gray metal desks. The windows on the wall directly behind the desks were covered by partially opened Venetian blinds, the weak morning sun filtering through the slats onto the gritty linoleum floor. To the extreme left of the room stood a long cabinet and desk, Elliott Raven's domain. The cabinet contained the bulky radio and telephones that comprised the woefully out-of-date com line. The desktop was a mare's nest of thick books and papers.

The wall to the right of the counter had no windows, as on the other side of the wall was the game wardens' haunt. This dividing wall was decorated with the obligatory Chippewa Nation Seal, framed photographs of Tribal Chairman Perry Frenchette and Vice Chairman Amos Baptiste, a group photo of the current ruling council members, and a shot of David dressed in a suit, white shirt, and tie.

Appropriately, next to David's framed photo was a huge cork bulletin board littered with Wanted posters. The entire room was illuminated twenty-four hours a day by ceiling-hung fluorescent lights concealed under aged opaque plastic squares. To the extreme right was the door to David's cramped office, which also doubled—when needs must—as an interrogation room.

"Man, am I glad you're here!" Elliott exclaimed. "Frenchette's screamin' his guts out. He's been callin' here every five seconds." The phone began to ring. Elliott glared at the phone.

"I just know that's him. You get it. I don't think he likes me. And unlike some..."—he eyed David meaningfully—"I voted for him."

David went for the telephone on the counter while Elliott checked on the progress of the coffeepot. As he lifted the receiver David heard the voice of the Tribal Chairman. The man sounded as if he were on the verge of a stroke.

"Would you mind explaining just what you're doing over there when I specifically told that chucklehead to direct you straight to the courthouse?"

"Uhh, officers were dispatched—"

"Yes!" the chairman snapped. "They're here right now. What I'm calling to find out is just where the hell my personally appointed police chief might be!" In a lowered, menacing tone, he said, "You're making me look like a fool, David. And as you well know, I'm not the sort to forget anyone who makes me look like a fool."

What David wanted to say was "It's not even eight-thirty. What the hell are you doing at the courthouse this early?" What he said was "I'll be right over."

"I hope you're awake enough to remember to call Bayfield County." On that sarcastic note, the Tribal Chairman slammed down the phone.

David no longer needed Elliott to tell him all that much. Which was good, because his dispatcher could handle only one thing at a time. At that moment Elliott was mentally and emotionally involved with the percolator, busily jiggling the cord in an all-out effort to encourage the appliance to accept electrical juice from the wall socket. One of these days they would throw the fixed budget to the wind and raid petty cash. Still, badly as his department needed something a bit more modern and reliable, today was not a good day to yearn for a new coffeemaker. If Perry Frenchette was anxious to have Bayfield County called in, that could mean only a major infraction of rez and civil law. And at the Tribal Courthouse, of all places.

David punched in the number. After two rings he heard, "Bayfield County Sheriff. How may I help you." The latter was not a question, merely the end of a wearily delivered opener.

"Yeah, this is Police Chief Lameraux over here in Red Cliff. We have a felony."

Completely interested now, the deputy sat straight up in the chair, gripped the receiver tightly with one hand as the other scrambled to find a usable pen lurking somewhere in his desk drawer. Finding one, then rapidly running the tip back and forth over the blotter to make certain the ballpoint had ink, he said crisply, "Exact location?"

"Tribal Courthouse just off Highway 13."

"Exact nature of the crime?"

Oops. David recovered quickly. "Hang on for a second. My other line's ringing." He pushed the Hold button, turned, and yelled at Elliott: "Did Perry bother to say what the hell happened?"

Beaming with pride now that the percolator was finally making a satisfactory *ploop, ploop* sound, Elliott replied, "He didn't need to. His sister-in-law Thelma told me straight from the get-go. It was her that found Judah Boiseneau with his brains blown out."

"Ho-wah!" (Untranslatable.)

Elliott wasn't finished. "According to Thelma, Benny did the shootin'."

"Benny Peliquin?" David cried.

"That'd be him. Thelma said Benny showed up at the office late last night and that him an' Jud started in to having a big old yelling fight. Got real ugly, so she left."

Fuming, David yelled, "I wish you'd told me even just a little bit of this before I started fumble-gumming with Bayfield."

"Well, I didn't know you was callin' 'em, did I?"

Elliott's form of logic was just a little too tough to tackle first thing in the morning. Gazing at his dispatcher with a thoroughly beaten expression, David sighed and responded, "Elliott, get on the horn and call Mel. Tell him to get over to Benny's and pick him up."

Elliott hurried to his desk, sat down to go to work on the com line. David went back on the line, sounding just as official as he could manage.

"What we have is a homicide. The victim is male, early thirties. His name is Judah Boiseneau and he was employed as our tribal attorney. He was killed in his office and discovered this a.m. by Mrs. Thelma Frenchette. I have two officers on site keeping the crime scene intact. Mrs. Frenchette has also named a possible."

"And can I have that name?"

"Hey," David replied cheerily, "you sure can." But without giving the name, a tactic intended to ensure that someone from Bayfield County actually put in an appearance, David hung up.

In Washburn, Michael Bjorke, only recently arrived from Madison, looked at the receiver in his hand and swore a blue streak. Meanwhile, Elliott Raven was pouring steaming brew into a Styrofoam cup and then passing it to Police Chief David Lameraux as David turned away from the counter.

DAVID KEPT HIS head down as he walked across the lot carrying his second cup of coffee of the day. He passed by the game wardens as they stood, arms folded across their chests, their interest riveted on the doings just over the little footbridge spanning the narrow creek that separated the parking lot for the Tribal Courthouse from that for the police/game warden department. The tribal ambulance was already in the other lot and pedestrian traffic was becoming brisk as people living in houses just across the way scooted back and forth from their homes to the courthouse trying to find out what was going on. From seemingly nowhere, folks who didn't live anywhere in the immediate area were trotting across Blueberry Road in the hopes of having a gander, too. Boy-hidey. This morning's activity sure beat the boogers out of the excitement generated a couple of weeks ago when a light plane put down on Highway 13. Lucky for the pilot that stretch was fairly straight and relatively untraveled at three in the afternoon. Otherwise...well, no one could really think of a really good otherwise.

THREE

RICHARD BLANKENSHIP, M.D., born and bred on the Cherokee reservation in North Carolina, came to the small hospital on Red Cliff rez a decade earlier. Unlike the thoroughly modern and touristy Cherokee rez, Red Cliff had no neon signs, fast-food outlets, or hotels. Ricky Blankenship fell in love with Red Cliff for all of these reasons. The remoteness of the reservation worked to make Red Cliff one of the few unspoiled sections left in Indian Country. Remoteness and unspoiled scenic beauty suited Doc Ricky right down to his toes. After ten years, first as an intern, then as a staff doctor, Ricky became chief of staff.

Being chief of staff meant that when he wasn't treating an overabundance of patients or acting as the lone medical examiner, he also worked the telephones, recruiting likely interns right out of med schools. Doc Ricky had to beat the bushes on a close-to-daily basis, as newly ordained doctors had a tendency to come and then go the very day their six months were up. Doctoring Indians looked a heck of a lot better on a résumé than it was in actual practice, largely due to the quirk that even when sick or in pain, Indians don't like to complain—most especially to someone they don't know. This characteristic creates the worst patients ever known to Hippocrates. In the main, Indians going to a rez clinic must persevere until they are rewarded with a turn at a doctor. Then when their turn comes, they invariably sit like brooding lumps fully expecting that if the doctor is any good at all, he will be able to guess what's wrong. Unfortunately, med schools aren't in the business of cranking out good guessers, and as a result, non-Indian interns working for the Indian Health Services typically count the days and hours until they are free to flee the reservation.

To his tremendous relief Doc Ricky has never needed to recruit nurses, as a host of Chippewa women from Red Cliff and the surrounding Ojibway reservations are fully licensed RNs. There were an equal number still in training. And every last one of them wanted to work on her home reservation. The blessing was, Chippewa nurses weren't in medicine to make big money, have a career. They didn't mind the low pay or the long hours, as these women had gone off to nursing schools with the sole aim of giving back to their communities. Which made them excellent nurses. And when assisting a new staff intern thoroughly baffled by his first stone-silent Indian patient, great guessers.

A tall, stringy man, Richard Blankenship was nearly as blind as a black water turtle, unable, without thickly lensed glasses, to see anything beyond a blur. He was a good doctor with an incredibly busy life that made him habitually late for absolutely everything. Everyone on Red Cliff swore by Doc Ricky, were willing to wait in the clinic for as long as it took in order to have five minutes of the man's time. Because Doc Ricky was a Shinabe, an Indian, he was the only doctor in the clinic able to look into his patients' eyes, ears, noses, and throats and know the medicines that would make them feel better. All those young Chamook doctors knew how to do was talk, talk, talk.

But dealing with violent death, most notably a murder...well, the whole thing made Doc Ricky nervous as hell. And when he was nervous, Doc Ricky could be something of a wild card.

DOC RICKY WAS an entire pack of wild cards just at the moment, and because of this, the second he was escorted by a policeman back down the hallway and into the reception area of the courthouse, two secretaries were prepared to grab and mother the whey out of him, bringing him coffee, even allowing him to smoke, an action the two women under normal circumstances absolutely forbade. But Doc Ricky'd had a nasty shock, and God knew this wasn't a normal morning. Once Doc Ricky was settled, the two went back to giving short shrift to the multitude of telephone callers. The secretaries weren't allowed to talk about what was going on, and besides, with David Lameraux in the room, they'd rather look at him than talk on the phone anyway.

If ever there was a man born to melt female hearts, David Lameraux was that man. What made him infinitely more attractive was his obliviousness to his own good looks. In cowboy boots and tight jeans he looked even taller than he actually was, and as the two women allowed their gaze to linger on his wonderfully tight behind, their hands unconsciously fanned deeply flushed faces.

Tribal Chairman Perry Frenchette had David off in the far corner, giving him a healthy dose of his opinion, while apart from them Ricky sat sipping coffee, happily smoking one cigarette after another. It was supposed to be a private telling-off, but with over half of the building closed until the Bayfield County sheriff's department arrived, there wasn't any space for a private anything. So of course the two secretaries and Doc Ricky heard everything Perry had to say. Primarily because they were listening intently.

"I'm more than a little distressed by your lackadaisical attitude," the chairman said flatly. "We have a murder and you just come moseying in here—"

"I moseyed?" David echoed, eyebrows raised.

Frenchette went on as if he hadn't noticed David's response. "…wearing jeans and that damn baseball cap. And when are you going to get yourself a haircut? Regulations state that a policeman's hair is suppose to be *above* the collar. You promised you'd have your hair cut, but as anyone can plainly see, it's still hanging in a ponytail halfway down your back. You're completely out of uniform, Lameraux. And that's just what the Bayfield officers will think the second they clamp eyes on you." The chairman exhaled deeply. He was winding down. "This is my last warning. If you don't straighten up, you're going to find yourself out of a job."

David shoved his hands deep into his jean pockets. Coldly eyeing the chairman, he said evenly, "You want my job, Perry? Hey, you got it. No need to hem and haw. Just go ahead and speak right up."

Frustration evident, Perry Frenchette cried, "Damn you—"

David drew his hand out like a gun, index finger solidly pressing against the shorter man's chest. "No! Damn you for always putting the police department last. You can install new carpeting in all the tribal buildings, but you can't spare a dime for the P.D."

The chairman's mouth tightened and he jutted out his chin. "The P.D. is practically moot. We have no crime here!"

"Well we have one now!" David scoffed. "And from what I hear, it's a real beaut."

The chairman flicked a tongue over dry lips. Resorting to IBM stuffy, he came back with "I have no intention of standing around here arguing the budget. What I expect is that you get on with your job and that you do that job in the most professional manner possible."

"Of course you do." David was quick to agree. "But just now I can't do squat until Bayfield County decides to do me the tremendous favor of poppin' on by. And you expect me to play dress-up for that bunch?" David sent the chairman a scathing look. "Man, that'll be the day. I stay just as I am or you put out your hand for my badge. It's your choice, Perry."

His face red with anger, Perry Frenchette spun on his heel, storming off along the corridor. Everyone heard the door of the office he'd commandeered slam, felt the walls quake. When David turned his head, the secretaries in the reception triangle suddenly became very busy. With the blasted phones ringing down the ceiling, appearing busy wasn't hard. But David knew every word that had been traded between himself and the chairman had been heard and soaked up faster than a biscuit sopping gravy. It was also a certainty that as soon as he went off down the hall, was out of earshot, the fleet-footed Moccasin Telegraph would again be sent into action.

His temper getting the better of him, he shouted for the doctor, causing Dr. Richard Blankenship to bolt out of the hard plastic chair. In the process he dropped his cigarette and sloshed coffee all over himself, the affected sections of the light cotton slime-green scrubs immediately turning black. Doc Ricky wasn't concerned about his scrubs; he was too busy trying to snatch up the cigarette before it could do permanent damage to the expensive new carpeting. Ricky was still fumbling when the secretaries came on the trot. David quickly rescued the hapless doctor from their wrath, grabbing him by the upper arm, propelling him toward the door.

Outside on the cement stoop, now awash with morning sunshine, Ricky looked about for a suitable repository for the cigarette butt and the cup. There wasn't one. He settled for simply dropping the butt into the dregs of the coffee, then setting the cup close to the edge of the stoop. Still holding the doctor's arm, David led him away from the front door, into the full blaze of the morning light. Before he had the chance to speak, a dusty tan sedan bumped into the lot and screeched to a stop. Front and back doors popped open and three men folded out.

The BIA was now officially on the scene.

Two white men fell in behind C. Clarence Begay, the head agent generally referred to as the Navajo.

As the parade passed them by, C. Clarence acknowledged the police chief and the doctor with a grunt and a nod. And kept on moving. Not until the three BIAers disappeared inside did David return his attention to the doctor.

"Talk to me about our victim."

Doc Ricky fiddled with an empty pack of cigarettes, index finger shoved inside the top opening, fruitlessly rooting for one last cigarette. Pulling a face, David removed a hard pack of Marlboros from his shirt pocket, shook out two, passed one to Ricky. The doctor's hands trembled as he tried to light it. Having already lit his own, David passed the Bic's flame Ricky's way. The two of them stood for a moment, inhaling and exhaling smoke. When the doctor decided to speak, he answered in totally Wild Card Ricky.

"Well, simply from cursory exam I'd have to say that poor Jud is dead."

At least he hadn't sung the *Oklahoma* show tune, and for that David was grateful. "Droll, Rick. Really droll."

Doc Ricky was chugging another drag, smoke billowing from his mouth. "Hey, *s-gi*. I do my best."

David canted his head, squinting at the doctor. "How long have you been in these woods?"

"Give or take a decade?"

"Yup."

"A decade."

"And you're still clinging to the Eastern Cherokee way of saying thank-you?"

Doc Ricky's magnified eyes swam behind the Coke-bottle lenses, looking all the world like a pair of dark fish bumping against the glass of their twin tanks. "Well, excuse the linguistic breath out of me. Possibly you haven't noticed, but I'm having a bad day."

David placed a hand on the other man's shoulder. "We all are, Rick, but I need you to stay with me a few minutes longer. Then you can go some place dark and quiet and have yourself a nice little nervous breakdown."

"Swear?"

"Yup."

The amplified eyes became partially hidden as the doctor squinted, suspicious. "Just how legally binding is a *yup?*"

David's hand left the doctor's shoulder, a frown conveying that he'd reached dark-humor overload.

"Okay, okay." Ricky sighed. He took another deep draw from the cigarette, exhaled, strove for a more professional tone. "Jud was shot in the side of the head at close range."

"How close is close?"

"Hugging close. As in tight hug. There's no exit wound, which means the bullet zinged around inside his skull until solid gray matter was reduced to linguini."

"I take it his death was instantaneous."

"Oooooh, you betch'um." Ricky could maintain professional detachment for only so long. In this instance, a whopping whole minute.

David turned at the waist, teeth scraping the corner of his mouth as he studied the courthouse. "I guess I've put it off for as long as I can. I've gotta go back in there and take a look at our victim."

"Better you than me."

David turned quickly, staring for a long moment at the medical examiner. "Rick," he said in a low voice, "you're a doctor. The sight of blood isn't suppose to affect you."

"Yeah? Well, looking at a corpse that was once the father of the two kids I've treated for flu and ear infections makes me a bad, bad M.E."

Looking up at the sky, David shook his head. "Naaah. That just makes you a little too sensitive."

With Ricky in reluctant tow, David paused at the reception counter, speaking to one of the attentive ladies. "Has the widow been located yet?"

Aggie Primeaux breathlessly spoke right up. "We're still trying to find her. She's not answering at the house."

"Maybe she drove her kids to school. Call over there and ask the principal to do his best to find her for me."

"I'll get right to it."

David's knuckles rapped the countertop. "Good girl."

Aggie Primeaux was a bit long in the tooth to be considered a girl, good or otherwise. But that the gorgeous Police Chief Lameraux would think so had her giggling as she punched the number for the elementary school in Bayfield.

TRIBAL CHAIRMAN Perry Frenchette was holed up in the Tribal Judge's office with the BIA boys, the office door closed. Even through wood, as David passed that door he clearly heard raised voices, the loudest, the Navajo's.

"Damn it, Frenchette! Not only do I have the right, I have the authority…"

David and Ricky continued on down the corridor, coming to the two officers standing guard just outside an open door. The youngest officer, Melvin Paris, looked keyed. "This is some kinda morning, eh, boss?"

"You might want to bring down your excitement a little," David said, his disapproval evident. Removing his baseball cap, holding it in one hand, David leaned in the doorway. The attorney's office wasn't large. A bulky wooden desk, shoved tight against the left wall, still managed to take up most of the floor space. Because it was an end office, two windows were set into the right wall. Behind the desk was a freestanding bookcase jammed with law

books and bound tribal treaties, each volume im-
printed with the relevant years, beginning with the
late 1700s and advancing steadily onward. To the
side of the book cabinet and fixed to the bare cream-
colored wall with pushpins was a large map of Red
Cliff. Lastly, half hidden by the bulk of the desk,
lying facedown and crumpled on the floor like a pile
of discarded clothing, was the mortal coil of Judah
Boiseneau.

A strong coppery odor wafted out to David as he
silently studied the large stain on the new carpet that
surrounded the dead man's head like a black halo.
The stain pattern told David that death had not been
immediate. The bullet had turned Jud into vegetable
instantly, but some part of his brain had survived a
second or two, keeping the heart muscle pumping
following the collapse to the floor. He asked his officers in a half whisper, "You guys keeping everybody out of here?"

"We've been trying," Melvin replied. "But trying to stop the Navajo was like trying to stop a
windstorm. He just went on in. He was stomping all
over the place when Perry finally ordered his fat butt
out."

Great, David thought angrily. Keeping this crime
scene intact was about as simple as hitting the moon
with a load of buckshot. David vented his frustration
on the doctor. "And how about you, Rick? Did you

wear gloves the entire time you were doin' your thing?''

"No. Not until I actually worked on the body."

David felt his blood pressure rising. "Why not?"

"I guess because as a general rule, dead guys aren't all that fussy about germs."

Doc Ricky was beginning to irritate the living fire out of David. Shoving the doctor forward he said sourly, "Okay, it's show-and-tell time. I want you to point to anything you might have touched before you started in on Jud."

"How the hell am I suppose to remember that?" Ricky cried.

"You wanna be a suspect?"

"No."

"Then if I were you, I'd get to remembering all your touchy, feely places pretty damn fast."

"Ahh, shit!"

AGGIE PRIMEAUX DID MORE talking than requested. Well, she'd had to. The school secretary was a cousin, and when her cousin asked, "What's going on, Aggie?" the question operated like pressure on a fault line. Aggie dutifully opened up like the San Andreas. Later she was put on hold, waiting while her cousin tracked down the principal. It was a while before the principal came on the line, and Aggie once again said much more than had been requested by Police Chief Lameraux. Alarmed, the elementary school principal hung up, running to search the hallways for Mrs. Boiseneau.

The first bell for class sounded shrilly, the principal maneuvering his way through waves of children running for their classes. Teachers were closing the classroom doors. The principal quickly motioned to the teachers who happened to notice him to come forward. The three teachers were stunned by the news of Judah Boiseneau's untimely demise. But not so shocked as to be at a loss for an opinion.

"I knew something like this was going to happen," one said sharply. "I just thought it would be *him* shooting her."

The principal was caught off balance by the acerbic remark. "Are you talking about *Mrs.* Boiseneau?"

The three women looked at each other; then, as if reluctant, they nodded.

The principal gasped sharply. "Why on earth would any of you think something so terrible?"

The teachers looked astonished. Finally, one put voice to the astonishment. "You mean…you don't know?"

DEPUTY MICHAEL BJORKE drove U.S. 13 from Washburn along the two-lane route that curved out of Chequamegan Bay and hugged the coastline of the peninsula jutting into Lake Superior. A hard-core city boy, he was not moved by the sight of old farms intermixed with forests. Michael was also fighting a rumbling stomach, the by-product of a bachelor's breakfast. In the backseat of the blue-gray Ford sedan were the two crime-scene technicians. Riding shotgun was long-time Republican Sheriff Ralph T. Bothwell. The two crime-scene guys were around the same age as Michael, meaning barely a hiccup over thirty. Ole Bothie teetered on the brink of retirement. In Michael's opinion Ole Bothie's retirement was long overdue.

Bothwell's sluggish style of crime busting was responsible for holding up the parade to the reservation. Michael and the crime guys had been ready to go from the time the Indian cop had hung up on him, yet they'd had to cool their jets for a good half hour waiting for Bothie. And then the sheriff had wanted to stop for breakfast!

In the hopes that the corpse would still be vaguely fresh when they got there, Michael had stopped at a convenience store and bought candy bars. Which was why he was now regretting the Butterfinger, learning to his great dismay that chocolate-covered peanut-butter crunchy stuff and a dippy two-laner were not a happy mix. Especially as every now and again Bothwell would indent his side of the car seat and cut one, the smell coming out of that man, inhuman. Michael hated his new boss and knew for a certainty that despite Bothwell's jocularity, the feeling was mutual.

Bothwell was not happy about Michael's transfer to his department. Not happy at all. But being a political animal Bothwell knew he could not say no when the hard currency of politics—personal favors—was in play. Accepting Michael Bjorke as a deputy was definitely a personal favor. One he owed to the lieutenant governor, no less.

Deputy Bjorke's maternal uncle.

"He's a good cop, but for now, it would be best if he were not in Madison. A year ought to do it. I'm trusting you to take good care of him."

Bothwell was taking very good care of *Mikey*. He had him answering the phones. Casting "Politico Boy" in a demeaning job had proven quite satisfying. At least until this morning. It had been the sheriff's bad luck that there had been no one else in the office to field the call from the rez. Then Mikey, bone-weary of desk duty, had had the audacity to cite the reg stating that any field-qualified officer answering such a call meant that said case automatically belonged to him. Still more than a little peeved, Bothwell treated his new deputy to yet another S.B.D.

THE MOCCASIN TELEGRAPH hadn't quite made it to Little Sand Bay Road, and Tracker was one of the few Indians still drawing breath who didn't own a scanner. Totally unaware of the murder, she was in her truck heading for the Native Spirit Gifts, the rez

gift shop and local outlet for her innovative style of
pottery. A highly skilled sculptor, she began with an
ordinary pot. Then, using her fist, she caved in one
side of the wet pot, filling in the created space with
a sculpted face. Every face appearing from the side
of one of her pots was haunting and undeniably
Chippewa. Her work was also sold out of a gallery
in Minneapolis—the same gallery that hadn't
wanted her when she'd been a starving art student.

At least the lady manager hadn't wanted her.
"My dear," the woman had said, elongating the
dear as if she were the owner of a general store and
speaking to a poor Indian waif begging for a penny
gum ball. "Have you even the faintest idea how
many potters there are in the Twin Cities area?"

Knowing the question was rhetorical, Tracker remained mute, seeing only peripherally the man to
her left.

The woman continued, tingeing her voice with a
note of regret. "And all of them are professionals,
artists with years of experience and...verve. Oh,"
she hastened to add, "I'm not saying you're without
talent. There is a certain value in your effort. But
perhaps with a bit more maturity and—"

Suddenly the shadowy man was just there, star-
tling them both as he removed a pot from the heavy
cardboard box Tracker held in her arms. He handled
it carefully, examining it. He'd picked out the first

pot she had ever created with a face peeking out from the indented side.

"This is marvelous. What an addition to my collection," the man had said, his voice warm and mellow. "That is, if I'm not too immature to offer for it?"

Another rhetorical. The man's hair was gray. The manager's eyes flared with horrified surprise. "Why, why of course, Mr. Heist," she stammered. "That's the very piece I would have chosen if not—"

Tucking the pot into the crook of his arm, Mr. Heist raised a silencing hand. "Yes, if not for the fact you must daily turn away dozens of more experienced potters."

The woman attempted a smile, her entire face stiff with the effort. Mr. Heist paid two hundred and fifty dollars for the pot. The three remaining pots were taken by the manager on consignment and Tracker dared hope that as an artist, she was on her way to success. The aforementioned lady manager was definitely on her way. But just to where wasn't clear. All Tracker was told by Harold Arnold, the gallery owner, was that his former manager had decided to move on.

Tracker liked dealing strictly with Harold, or Harry, as he called himself. He was short and Jewish—"Tribe of Levi," he chortled—and she trusted him absolutely to get the best possible prices for her labors. On the home front, Native Spirit Gifts was running a close second to the sales volume of Minneapolis. And Tracker's success was due to the faces. Or more correctly, to the one face she could not stop her fingers from sculpting. The one face that was there each and every night, hovering above her like a phantom lover.

Which was entirely appropriate.

FOUR

PURELY OUT OF GUILT for having yelled at her dog, Tracker made pancakes, Mushy's favorite breakfast. Now he was having the time of his life, hanging out of the truck's passenger window, the wind whipping pelt, ears, and tongue. Because of the winds barreling off the lake, Tracker was wearing a jacket, flannel shirt, thick socks, and jeans. A mere ten-minute drive inland and spring's mild heat was enveloping her.

Blueberry Road is the official rez through road, zigging through the center of the tiny town, then skirting the boundary of the reservation. A minute after turning onto Blueberry, Tracker remembered that Uncle Bert wasn't doing well—flu or something. Her father had made it quite clear that as she lived closer to her uncle than anyone else in the family, he expected her to do her bit in checking on the old man. Uncle Bert's home was in the forested cove of Raspberry Bay. He had no neighbors, no telephone.

Tracker dreaded having to make the house call.

Uncle Bert had been the family hermit for nearly fifteen years. Uncle Bert was stone deaf, and because of his affliction, ornery. Hence the hermit thing. But he was alone and ailing, so like it or not, he was about to have a visit from his nearest neighbor/relative. Uncle Bert wouldn't like it. Nor would his collection of cantankerous dogs. That thought caused her to stop the truck just after turning onto the dirt track that was Raspberry Road.

"Quit whining," she said sharply. She reached around Mushy's bulk and proceeded to crank up the window. "The last time we were here and the window was down, you jumped out and found yourself in a fight. A fight you weren't winning, remember?"

Mushy remembered. But the need for revenge had the big dog squirming and whining against the closed window. By the time the truck neared Uncle Bert's land assignment, Mushy was a quivering mass of muscle, his ruff standing straight up, a warning growl issuing from his throat. Mushy's way of declaring *Just let me at 'em. I know I can take 'em this time.*

Uncle Bert's front yard and his trailer with its long walled lean-to was a bleeding eyesore. Two years ago, attempting to spruce the trailer house up a bit, Uncle Bert began painting the thing a shade of crap green. Possibly because he hoped a green trailer in the woods would be an invisible trailer. Trouble was, he'd had only one bucket of the stuff.

He ran out of paint, then couldn't be bothered to buy more. The lingering effect was a thoroughly streaked green section on a faded blue and rust-splotched fifty-by-ten trailer. The logged wall lean-to looked good, though.

The yard was two parts au naturel and one part messy old man. Shutting down the truck's engine, Tracker waited for the hounds of hell to come bolting out, baying and snarling. But this morning the dogs were unusually tardy. As she waited in safety inside the truck, she began to notice the eerie silence. Then too, the old trailer seemed to sag more than normal, as if it had been...abandoned. Tracker instantly tossed the thought aside. Uncle Bert had lived on this assignment since Moses was a boy, first in a plank cabin that had eventually fallen down around his ears, then in the trailer—a gift from the tribe—back in the days when the trailer had been brand spanking new. Uncle Bert would never abandon his private chunk of forest.

Absolutely never.

"He's got to be running bears," Tracker mused aloud. Being Bear Clan, Uncle Bert wouldn't ever intentionally kill a bear. But that little taboo never stopped him or his dogs from trying to run the legs off the bears. Anticipating the imminent return of Uncle Bert and his pack of slathering mongrels, Tracker knew it would be best if she just stayed put. Which meant—hey! Ciggie time. Snapping off the shoulder belt she reached for the glove compartment, extracting the box of Marlboro Ultra Lights.

Tracker had been a smoker since she was thirteen. Not a heavy smoker, but a smoker nonetheless. And now that she lived like a cloistered nun, rarely drank, certainly didn't overeat, what else was there? Lighting up, she tried to ignore the almost sinister silence. Come to think of it, Mushy was a bit too quiet. Her eyes flicked in the dog's direction. Mushy was perfectly still, watching through the window, ruff smooth and flat. All very un-Mushy-like. But then, the hush hanging over this neck of the woods was equally unlike Uncle Bert.

Finally, cigarette smoked down to the filter, she stabbed it out in the ashtray and ordered Mushy to stay. Still leery of the hell hounds, she opened the cab door.

SECONDS AFTER she opened the unlocked door, she was engulfed by a stench emanating from the trailer's central area. Coughing, waving a hand in front of her face in an attempt to fan up a whiff of clean air, she entered the gloomy interior. Uncle Bert did have electricity, but because of the darkness, locating a light switch was as difficult as selecting a particular raindrop in a downpour. Uncle Bert had never been one for windows. Every window on the trailer was boarded over from the inside. He maintained that when he wanted to enjoy the beauty of the day he'd go outside. Actually, what he didn't like was the thought that anyone driving along Raspberry at night would see his lights. As he so quaintly put it, ''Folks comin to see ya in the dead of night only want one of two things: either to rob ya or to ask for a loan. Either way, you're out money.''

In this case, his boarded-over windows did more than keep daylight out. They trapped the smell inside. Unable to stand it, she fled, retiring to the rickety porch. She knew she couldn't just leave the situation like this. Her uncle might be in there dead or close to it. But the thought of groping around in the dark while the stench of the place permeated her clothing, skin, and hair caused her to shudder. Then she remembered the portable spotlight.

Ignoring Mushy's high-pitched pleas she rooted around in the extended cab until she found the portable spotlight, an item useful when hunting deer. That is, if Tracker's way of taking a deer could be glorified with the term *hunting*. Deer were everywhere, and taking one typically meant stopping the truck, popping on the light just long enough to get a fix, then shooting right out the truck window. After that, all that was left to do was to heft the carcass into the flatbed. On the rez, especially on Elderly Hunt Day, the meat processor who worked for free for that one day only knew immediately those who'd been former poachers and those who, because of the loosening of the gaming laws, had never needed to poach. Ex-poachers shot the deer in the neck, dropping it where it stood. Other hunters hit the deer in the shoulder, a bigger target.

Tracker was a neck shooter—one of the precious few *neckers* too young to have seen the inside of Bayfield County Jail.

Back inside the trailer, Tracker shone the spot around, finding at once the cause for the stink: trout, two strings rotting on the card table Uncle Bert used for everything, including dining. Judging from the condition of the fish, they'd been awaiting the gutting knife for at least three days. She whipped the beam away from the card table, scanning the living room. A heavy layer of dog hair coated everything, even the walls. Wading through the debris covering the floor, she inched forward. The thought of what she might find in the trailer's only bedroom had her heart hammering against her ribs.

TRAVELING TO TULSA from Duluth wasn't quite the snap Imogen's father had made it sound. Imogen knew this, having made the trip a dozen or more times. But during those past trips, Jud had been there to help—that is, when he'd taken it into his head to help. Now she was completely on her own, scared out of her wits, and frustrated by the Duluth International (flights into Canada qualified as International) Airport way of doing things.

Or not doing them.

The tickets had been waiting for her at the counter just as her father had promised. The trouble was, there weren't any flights until the following morning. Which meant Imogen had to bundle the children off to the Holiday Inn on Second Street, where she spent the night watching her children sleep. In those hours, the events of the last day replayed in her head like an exceptionally awful horror movie. Plate in hand, she'd gone to her husband's office to deliver his supper. The minute she stepped into the building she'd felt an odd foreboding. Shaken by what she could describe only as an unknown menace, she walked the corridor, pausing before the closed door of her husband's office. "Don't go in there!" she imagined a matinee audience screaming. Yet like the stiletto-wearing B-movie heroine who invariably twists her ankle when she runs away from the monster, Imogen had turned the knob. And then she'd heard her own screams.

Benny Peliquin was Jud's cousin. That was all he'd been to her for many years. When the trouble in her marriage escalated, became physical, Benny became her white knight, the man she could call any hour of the night or day. The only man in Jud's family willing to step between her and Jud's fists. In the past few months he underwent another transformation, becoming her gentle lover. The man responsible for the unborn child sleeping snug inside her womb. She shouldn't have told him. She really shouldn't have. Her confession to Benny had only expanded the fierce tensions, Jud's reactionary violence.

"You have to leave him, Jeanie. You have to come to me. You have to let me protect you."

"And who's going to protect us from the crap that will start flying around this rez?"

"Let me worry about that."

"No! Don't push me, Ben. Please, just don't push. I have to have time to think."

"And if Jud starts knocking you around while you're thinking? Am I suppose to just let that happen?"

"I'll call the cops."

Benny's mocking laugh had been hard. *"Yeah, like they're such a help."*

"But this time I'll file charges. I really will, Ben."

He'd merely looked at her, both of them knowing she wouldn't. Imogen preferred bruises to disgrace. Her father, the career politician, had taught her and her mother only too well that outward appearances to the voting public were absolutely everything. Which was why when Jud began knocking her around early in the morning, Imogen had done nothing more than yell to her children to run outside and hide. Once they were gone, she had done what she could to protect herself and her unborn baby from Jud's uncontrollable temper.

Now Jud was dead.

Given the fact that his unnatural demise had occurred just hours after their latest physical go-round, and knowing that on Red Cliff rez it would have taken less than an hour for Benny to have heard all about it, Imogen hardly required the services of Sherlock Holmes to work out this particular little whodunit. Which was why she was running. She couldn't allow her children to be caught up in the cross fire. She had to get them to safety. Then and only then would she come back—never mind that her father would forbid it—to stand by Benny's side. She owed him that. After all, he'd killed Jud in order to protect her.

Protect their baby.

Hadn't he?

THE FIVE-THIRTY wake-up call came, but Imogen hardly needed it. She roused the children and got them ready to face the Northwest puddle jumper, then the mad dash through the Minneapolis airport to make the connecting flight. With every nerve in her body buzzing, Imogen hustled the two children from one flight to the next, tried to coax them into eating airplane food, and then begged them to sit still during those moments they aggravated the other passengers. It wasn't until she and the children deplaned in Tulsa and she saw her father and mother waiting that Imogen finally allowed herself to cry.

DAVID'S ONLY REAL DUTY was to keep the crime scene intact. He also had to keep Doc Ricky halfway calm and in attendance. The latter was proving to be more difficult by the minute as Doc Ricky became increasingly insistent about leaving. He'd been on emergency duty all night long and this morning was expected at the well baby clinic. Doc Ricky's strong opinion was that his continuing attention to one dead man wasn't worth the health risk to even one live baby. The man had a valid point, but the Bayfield County coroner told David point-blank over the telephone that he felt no compunction to haul himself out to Red Cliff. "Hell, Rick's forgotten more about forensics than I'll ever know."

When David duly passed on the message that the coroner had lobbed the ball back into Ricky's court, Doc Ricky had turned sullen. Ricky's physician assistant would have to see to the babies. Ricky didn't care for that, and judging by the one-sided telephone conversation, Wanda, his assistant, wasn't especially thrilled either.

David had completely cordoned off the back of the building and dismissed all nonessential personnel. He hadn't really had the authority to give the staff a day off, but as the Tribal Chairman continued to confer behind closed doors, David had been left to assume that authority. Frenchette would most probably bust a gut when he poked his head out and realized that for all intents and purposes tribal employees were enjoying an unscheduled day off with full pay, but David couldn't do his job with a flock of onlookers sticking to him like gum.

Standing in the small parking lot staring at the tips of his boots, David listened to his officers. He was not pleased with what they had to say. "What do you mean, you can't find the widow?" He directed this question to his youngest patrolman, Melvin Paris.

"She's just...gone, David," Melvin whined. "When she didn't answer the doorbell, we broke in."

"Just on the off chance that whoever shot her husband had gotten her, too, right?"

"Yeah!" Mel agreed, taking his cue from David as to why he had broken down the Boiseneaus' front door. A bit more confident now, Mel went on with his account. "The station wagon she drives wasn't in the driveway, but that didn't mean anything. She coulda been laying on the living room floor just as dead as her husband, and the killer coulda stole her car. So we put our shoulders to the door, and after we were inside, we had a good look around." Melvin shook his head. "You wouldn't believe that place. Everything's so damn...neat. Kinda like folks didn't really live there, ya know? The beds were all made, no kids' stuff laying around, no dishes in the sink." Mel went quiet as he recalled the eat-off-the-floor quality of the Boiseneau home. Then he remembered the one thing out of keeping with the rest of the house.

Snapping his fingers, he blurted, "Hey, there was a covered plate of food on the kitchen table. Looked like Jud's supper. Kinda funny it wasn't in the oven. My mom always puts plates like that in the oven. So's the food'll stay warm."

As interesting as this was, David was more interested in the preservation of any and all scenes and evidence. "Did you leave everything just like you found it?"

"Yeah. Except for the door, we sure did, boss."

David turned his head away, thinking out loud. "If we can't locate the widow in an hour, I'll go over there and have a look at the house myself." As if coming back to himself David turned toward Joey Du Bey.

Joey was his most reliable officer, which meant he could depend on him to think on his own instead of calling in for further instructions. Now there was a handy attribute. The pity was, David and Joey disliked each other. Their animosity was strictly personal and both did their best to leave it outside the office, but too often it just cropped up.

"Benny's missing too?"

"Oh, you know it," Joey scoffed. "When I couldn't raise anyone inside his trailer house, I went over to Willard's." Joey didn't need to elaborate further on the reasoning behind this move. Benny was a fisherman, the boat he worked off belonging to his cousin Willard. "I talked to Debbie," Joey continued, meaning Willard's wife. "According to her, Willard's pretty pissed because he's got two gangs of nets out and Benny didn't show up to help with the lifting.

"The next thing I did was take a drive to the high school. I took Benny's son and daughter out of their classes and drove them home. Ben's daughter Pearl used her *key*." Joey emphasized the last word, intentionally pointing up the fact that he'd taken the preferred route of legal entry. "Pearl couldn't tell if anything was missing. Said she couldn't say if her dad had been home during the night or not. She did admit that she and her brother Darren had fixed their own supper and that their dad wasn't home when they went to bed about eleven. Pearl and Darren did insist that even though Benny's bedroom door was closed when they were getting dressed for school, they could hear him snoring. Then I asked if they thought he was sleeping regular or passed out drunk. The kids wouldn't answer me."

David's eyes narrowed. "Benny's not a hard drinker."

"He has been lately," Joey countered. "I saw him in the Lanes a couple of nights ago. He helped close the place. And he was hammered, David. I'm talkin' *real* hammered."

David leaned in, hollering at Joey. "And you let him drive!"

Joey answered just as loudly, his quick temper rising. "Your niece Tootie took his keys off him and drove him home in his truck while her boyfriend Mark followed in Tootie's car. It was all under control, David. I made sure of it."

David at once regretted his outburst. Throwing a tantrum in front of his other officers was a sure sign of weakness or jealousy. Once upon a time, Joey Du Bey had been a friend. In fact, David used to tease Joey about looking so much like Johnny Depp. But during the last year, it was all David could do not to drastically rearrange Joey's movie-star face. His tone flinty, he said, "What else do you have to tell me?"

Looking smug, Joey crossed his arms against his chest. "Just that I thought it would be better if Benny's kids stayed out of school for the rest of the day, so I left Rodney to keep an eye on them and to wait in case Benny turned up." Joey canted his head, his eyes narrowing. "This is lookin' kinda bad for old Ben, eh?"

Both men were separately walking the same trail, remembering not only the gossip concerning Benny and Imogen Boiseneau, but also those occasions when concerned neighbors had reported sounds of violence coming from the Boiseneau home. There hadn't been much the police who responded to the calls could do because Mrs. Boiseneau had always flatly refused to say anything beyond "I fell."

David remembered all of those pesky rumors linking Mrs. Boiseneau to Benny Peliquin. In the beginning, about a year ago, he'd treated the rumors as nothing more than good old rez gossip. Who wouldn't? Mrs. Boiseneau was half Benny's age and an attractive, university-educated lady. Benny Peliquin was as plain as Red Cliff dirt, a commercial fisherman and a widower with two half-grown kids. But the rumors had persisted, even intensified. And if Benny had been doing some hard drinking lately...

David stopped the thought cold. Sounding annoyed, he replied, "It's not looking that damn good."

"Uh-oh," Mel said. "They're here."

All heads turned as a blue-gray car turned into the Council Office parking lot. Almost forty minutes past their stated ETA, the Bayfield County sheriff and deputies were finally on the scene.

"Five bucks says they got lost," Mel offered.

No one covered his bet.

MICHAEL WHEELED INTO a vacant parking slot. The technicians piled out and were at the back of the car retrieving their work kits from the trunk before Michael had even killed the engine. Turning off the

ignition, he looked toward the group of Indian policemen. Four wore navy blue shirts and trousers,
gun belts, and regulation black boots. They were not
wearing hats. Neatly trimmed dark hair glinted blue
streaks everywhere the sunlight touched. The odd
man out was the officer standing head and shoulders
taller than the rest. He was wearing a policeman's
shirt tucked into faded jeans, brown cowboy boots,
and a navy blue Dukes baseball cap.

Go, northern bush leaguers, Michael thought with
a sneer.

"Looks like the gang's a-waitin'," Bothwell said.
He opened the car door, preparing to heave his bulk
out of the passenger side. "Yep, we got an ambulance, which means the M.E.'s on site, and over
there stands our red brother cops, every one of them
eagerly awaiting our wisdom." Bothwell looked
back over his sizable shoulder to Michael. His round
face broke into a smile. "And if you believe that
for a minute, I've got a mint-condition used car with
your name ready to go on the registration."

Michael placed a restraining hand on the other
man's shoulder. "I took the call, so this is officially
my investigation."

"Oooh, I wouldn't forget that for a minute, son.
In fact, just the heady anticipation of watching you
play big-city sleuth has me more excited than I've
been in years. If I didn't know better, I'd have said

I was damn near all atwit.'' Bothwell exited the car, tree-trunk-thick legs transporting him toward the waiting Indians.

GENERALLY, ALL THE Bayfield County guys looked alike. Same height and build and uniform, same vapid expression. During his first month as police chief, David had quickly realized that Sheriff Bothwell broke the mold—maybe due to his sheer volume. It had come as a bit of a relief that Bothwell was basically friendly. That certainly made it easier for David to work hand in glove with the Bayfield County department. So as Bothwell, hand extended, lumbered toward him, a smile on his wide face, David stepped away from his officers, smiled, and accepted the outstretched hand. Then his attention was diverted by the blond deputy hurrying to join them.

David's first impression was that the newcomer was a Wisconsin Swede, the kind likely to begin each sentence with *Ya sure* or *You betcha.* The clencher was the deputy's smile. The guy had three dimples, two dead center in the cheeks and a third just below the curve of his mouth. *A Viking son, by golly.*

The blond shook David's hand. ''Good morning, Chief.''

''Police chief,'' David replied coolly, retrieving his hand. ''I answer to David or, if you prefer, Police Chief Lameraux.''

''A Frenchy in the woodpile, eh?'' Michael was

now unsure of what to do with his hand after the Indian had roughly extracted his own. He allowed it to drift slowly down, settle at his side.

David knew the guy was just trying to make a friendly joke, but a man's ancestors were off-limits. Mentally David counted to five, then said casually, "Guess we're all a little Froggy around here." David turned to Bothwell. "Doc Ricky's been waiting for you to show up. I think he's smoked about a pack and a half by now."

Bothwell laughed, blithely ignoring the jibe that it had taken his department almost two hours to put in an appearance. "Hey, the doc's always at his best when he's stressed." Bothwell turned to Michael and explained. "Doc Ricky runs the rez hospital. He's also the best M.E. in four counties. The only fly in the ointment is, the doc hates dead people."

Michael's eyes were as blank as a cud-chewing cow's, but he nodded as if this information was useful.

Pushing the jacket of his suit back with his elbows, jamming his hands into his trouser pockets, Bothwell asked of David, "Is Gracie La Rue still cooking over at the Lanes?"

"Last time I looked."

Bothwell removed one hand from his pocket and patted the rounded belly straining the buttons of his regulation shirt. "Woman whips up the best breakfast in the world."

David grinned. "Yeah. Order one egg, you get three."

"Order an omelet, you get an even dozen." Bothwell issued a rolling laugh.

David laughed with him, knowing that Sheriff Bothwell was more than able to handle two of Gracie's whopper-sized omelets. "Talk to Doc Ricky first, then we'll get you fed."

Bothwell turned to Michael, clapping a hand on Michael's shoulder as he spoke to David. "This here's Deputy Bjorke."

Okay, David thought. *He's not a Swede, he's a Norskie* (Norwegian).

"He's the man who'll be handling the investigation. I'm only the ride along on this one."

Bothwell, watching the police chief's dark eyes, caught the snap of disapproval. The Shinabe police chief now blamed Michael for Bayfield County's tardiness. And Lameraux was the kind of guy who would make certain a report on that tardiness was filed with the state.

Cool.

Bothwell's smile widened. Despite the fact that he was famished, eager to sit down to one of Gracie La Rue's legendary omelets, the sudden prospect of watching the Indian cop lock antlers with the lieutenant governor's nephew promised to be terrific comic theater. The omelet could wait.

With a cheery cry of "Lead on MacLameraux,"

Bothwell, with Michael beside him, began following David toward the courthouse. Bothwell nudged Michael. "Ya know, judging from the way the introductions went, I'd say you two young fellas are gonna get along just great."

"YOU MEAN THAT CRAP Bothwell spouted was true?" Michael cried. "The M.E. really does have a phobia about dead bodies?"

David chewed the side of his cheek as he stared fixedly at the corridor's pine paneling. "What I'm trying to tell you," he said, enunciating carefully, "is that Dr. Blankenship doesn't normally deal with violent deaths, but he does know forensics, so you're damn lucky to have him. My advice is, try very hard not to piss him off."

Michael Bjorke wasn't very good at taking advice. Kneeling on the floor, his head less than an inch from Doc Ricky's, Michael examined the fatal wound to the victim's forehead. The Ex-Tribal Attorney's entire head was covered with a clear plastic bag secured to the neck with tape. The doctor's gloved hands were pressing the plastic against the head wound, so Michael had an unobstructed view of it.

"The barrel was against the skin," the doctor said.

Michael glanced at the M.E. "That close?"

Dr. Ricky nodded. "Oh, yeah. I need the microscope to place the barrel's depression for the purposes of technical evidence, but just with the naked eye you can see the gas spray.''

The blond man nodded as still on their knees they moved back from the body and each other. Doc Ricky began talking about types of gunshot wounds, bullet entrances and exits, shots at close range and long shots. Despite himself, Michael was enthralled. Never before had an M.E. actually talked to him. The M.E. in Madison had gone about his grim business, revealing little or nothing at all to the uniformed cops on the crime scene. A week later, the medical examiner made his final report to the detectives. And that was that. But this M.E. was a real motormouth, gesticulating with his hands as he spoke.

Hands that were no longer shaking.

''A bullet comes out with incredible speed. Faster than the speed of sound, really. The bang of a gun comes from the explosion in the barrel, not from the bullet. During the exit, the bullet takes all of the barrel explosion gases with it, and everything is spinning because of the ridges in the barrel. It's the spinning that makes the bullet fly straight. The ridges inside the barrel not only put a spin on the bullet, they groove a pattern into the slug, making firearm identification not only possible but thoroughly reliable.

''But back to target damage… When the bullet

strikes at close contact, all three layers of skin are affected by the gases right behind it. The bullet strikes first and then the gases hit. For about a millisecond the gases cause the skin to swell up like a balloon. A millisecond later, all three layers of skin just go *pop*. It's the popping that creates this blackened shredded trace. Under normal conditions, the bullet goes in clean, kinda like a drill. The mess a bullet makes tends to be on exit. The tissues, muscle, bone, and organs a bullet has to pass through slow it down, and a slowing bullet is an awkward rascal, tearing open a filthy hole on exit. I saw an upper leg once that from the front looked like the patient had a bee sting. The back of the leg, though, now that was unbelievable. The back of his leg looked like the guy sat down on a land mine."

Before the doctor could rattle on, Michael asked, "Okay, then why is the back of our guy's head so neat and clean?"

"Huh?" Pulled from his train of thought, Doc Ricky blinked several times, then simply stared vacuously from behind his thick lenses. It was like watching someone having a ministroke. Then he was back, just as crisp as a newly issued dollar bill. "Oh. That. Well, simply put, because the bullet's still in the noggin. It made a circular pattern in the skull until it ran out of steam and stopped. Which is good, because after I take it out, you'll have a spiffy match to the murder weapon."

Michael thought for a long moment as both men stared down on Judah Boiseneau's mortal remains. Behind them the two crime techs were working quietly and efficiently, one dusting for fingerprints with gray aluminum powder on light surfaces, white Lonconide on dark. The other was handling the camera, photographing the office from every possible angle. The camera flashed, then the automatic film advance purred. Besides bagging the victim's head, the doctor had also covered his hands, the plastic held in place by rubber bands around the wrists. Plastic bags also protected the victim's shod feet. The techs hadn't done the bagging. Doc Ricky had. Michael had to give the man credit for knowing just how to preserve evidence. But a nervous M.E. made Michael nervous. He could not afford a failure. Not if he wanted to get out of Bayfield County and back on the force in Madison.

"You have autopsy facilities here on Red Cliff?"

"We don't have the forensics specialists or the equipment you'll find in Green Bay," Doc Ricky admitted honestly. "But we are adequate."

Michael thought it over. The nearest hospital with proper morgue facilities was in Ashland. Transport would mean a rush by the rez ambulance up Highway 13, meeting the Ashland ambulance somewhere in the middle. The corpse would be moved into the second wagon, then taken to the larger hospital. A lot of time would be lost. Crucial evidence could very well be tainted.

Michael took a long look at the Indian doctor, noting the gaunt features, the nervous twitch of the mouth, the almost Asian cast to the dark eyes. He decided he simply couldn't afford to trust Doc Ricky.

"I believe I'd prefer Ashland."

The doctor looked openly hostile, then calmly said, "You got it." With that, he stood and peeled the disposable gloves from his hands while heading for the door. David blocked his exit, standing like a tree inside the door frame.

Ducking so that he was nearly eye level with Ricky and speaking in a voice too low to be normal yet too loud to be described as a murmur, David asked, *"Wegonen anin?"* (What's the matter?)

Chippewas point with their lips; Cherokees, with a lift of the chin. Lifting his chin in the blond man's direction, Ricky answered in a quiet voice and in perfect Ojibway. *"Nin angoa."*

Ricky tried to push on through, but David's bulk was in the way. His face full of anger, Ricky stared David down. This silent exchange lasted only a few seconds, just long enough for David to understand that this time good old Doc Ricky wasn't kidding around. Either David would move or Rick would find the strength needed to remove him. David chose to step out of the way, watching as the doctor strode off. After Ricky rounded the corner, David fixed his attention on the blond deputy. Bjorke hadn't seemed to register that he'd mortally offended Doc Ricky. Either that or the man simply didn't care.

Suspecting the latter and finding himself offended as well, David seethed. *"Ho-wah."* Motioning to Eric, the only officer left to guard the scene, to follow him, David stormed off. If the Bayfield County deputy wanted to play dirty, David could play dirty, too. And dirty in this instance meant leaving the Bayfield fool to worry about the crime scene all by his lonesome.

Meeting Bothwell in the center of the hallway, David passed him without a glance. The instant he and the officer turned the corner, Bothwell continued wandering down to the late attorney's office, poking his head through the open door. With a merry twinkle in his eyes and a grin the Cheshire Cat would envy, he called to Michael, "Well, looks like you've got our little collaboration off to a grand start. Good job, Mikey."

FIVE

C. CLARENCE BEGAY WAS so distressed he felt like he was dancing on a nail. Trapped in the public eye, he couldn't give in to the calming habit of chewing great holes into his knuckles. But he had to do something. Especially after being none too subtly dismissed by Frenchette. C. Clarence had every right and authority to sit in on the meeting between the Tribal Chairman and the Bayfield County sheriff. What C. Clarence hated most about Perry Frenchette was that the man wallowed in his own self-importance.

The truth as C. Clarence saw it was that Frenchette was little better than a jumped-up jack pine savage that no one outside of Wisconsin had even heard of. But in Indian Country—the *real* Indian Country—everyone knew C. Clarence Begay. Granted, his being a little *too* well known had bitten him in the ass—the primary reason he was doing mea culpa time in Wisconsin—but that was a side issue.

Reduced to prowling outside the courthouse like

a bloated cat, C. Clarence was smoking like a steam engine and trying not to dwell on the fact that the Bayfield County crime techs were taking apart Jud Boiseneau's office. If the techs came across that file and paused to read it, his best bet was to waste no time hotfooting it over into Canada. But if they should unearth the thing and simply toss it aside, he should also be near at hand to put the grab on it. The sheer uncertainty of it all, plus that little voice inside his head repeatedly advising him to run like the wind, had C. Clarence sweating buckets. He was relieved that his two assistants weren't around to witness his agitation. To spare himself that, he'd sent them off to fetch sandwiches and cold sodas. That little chore ought to keep them occupied for all of five minutes. After that, he didn't know what the hell to do about them. He shouldn't have brought them along. Then again, it would have looked suspect if he hadn't.

"I hate my life," he mourned, taking another long hit of nicotine.

DAVID PUSHED THROUGH the glass door, eyes glancing off the jittery BIA agent, settling on Joey, who was waving an arm inward, shouting, *"Wewibisi-win!"*

As requested, David began to hurry. As he was passing the BIA agent, the Navajo paused as if he were about to speak. Obviously thinking the better of it, the portly man continued pacing and puffing on a cigarette. Joey, standing near three police cruisers, seemed barely able to contain himself. David was only halfway across the parking lot when Joey began shouting the latest developments. "Benny was spotted!"

David picked up speed, running the remaining distance. Joey continued talking as David ran and was still talking when David arrived.

"Elliott's going nuts. Lots of calls coming in. Some of the calls were total crap, but everybody, and I mean everybody, knows we're huntin' Benny." Joey paused to take in a needed lungful of air. He ran a hand through his closely cropped black hair. "Anyway, Elliott got a call from Ned Girard. I can't remember all the details because you know how Elliott is when he's relaying information. I think you'd better talk to him."

David could have walked over to the station, but sliding inside one of the cruisers and using the radio was quicker. Sitting sideways on the driver's side, long legs hanging out of the opened door, David keyed the mike. "Elliott."

"Right here, boss."

"Talk to me about the call from Ned."

Elliott breathed heavily over the airwaves, his exasperation apparent. "It wasn't a call from Ned. I told Joey that. It was a call from Leroy Crane's wife Betty. You know her good, David. Remember when

Leroy bought her that fur coat after he won big at video poker? Well, Betty doesn't really wear the thing, but she worries about it plenty. Which is why she made Leroy put in one of those house alarms. Trouble is, half the time Betty forgets to turn the thing off. She's worse about it in the mornings. I blame the cat.''

David wiped away a trickle of sweat from his face, his expression pained. ''Elliott, is this information vital to the call about Benny?''

Elliott's response was brisk. ''I'm getting to that just as fast as I know how.'' Elliott cleared his throat over the airwaves. ''Betty slept in this morning and her cat was scratching at the door mouse—you know, one of those things made out of hemp rope that looks like a big mouse? She hangs it off the doorknob and the cat scratches at it whenever it wants to go outside. Betty claims she was still half asleep when she opened the door because that set off the alarm. Then that set Ned Girard's dog to howling, and the cat, who was already scared by the alarm bell, got more scared about Ned Girard's big old dog Brutus. Especially after that dog jumped the fence and chased the cat straight up into a tree.''

David keyed the mike, trying to cut in, but Elliott was relentless. The dispatcher ignored the clicking and kept right on talking. ''Well, Betty got real upset about her cat being in the tree. So upset that she was yelling at Ned and Ned's wife Irene. The three of them were having a big old over-the-fence fight and the alarm's still ringing. Which is why Betty's friend Clara Beauclaire, who lives just down the road, heard the alarm, and after five minutes of it still ringing, called in screaming that this time Betty was getting robbed for sure. So I sent Charlie to check it out.''

David finally got through. "Elliott?"

"Yeah, boss."

"Is there an end to this story? In my lifetime?"

"I told ya I'm gettin there!" The force of Elliott's tinny voice caused the radio speaker to vibrate. Having regained David's rapt attention, Elliott proceeded in a calmer tone. "Okay, so Charlie does the drive over, yeah? And according to him everything's just a shade crazy 'cause Betty's yelling at Ned, who's trying to control Brutus, and Irene Girard's yelling at Betty on account of Betty yelling at her husband, and the alarm's still going loud enough to be heard all the way over to the U.P., and the cat's way the hell up in the tree lookin' like it's about ready to jump to its death. First thing Charlie does is, he gets the alarm turned off and then he's gotta sort out the ugliness between Betty an' the Girards. It's after he gets everybody settled down that Ned tells him.''

David allowed Elliott two seconds worth of self-satisfaction. Then he keyed the mike, his voice utterly deadpan. "What did Ned tell Charlie, Elliott?"

"Huh? Oh." Elliott cleared his throat again. "Ned said his wife Irene had been walking their dog real early this morning, like about five, an' seen Benny's truck's over at the Boiseneaus' house. She said seemed to her that Benny was trying to look in one of the windows. When he spotted Irene, he ran and jumped in his truck and peeled out."

"He was at Jud's!" David cried.

"Yeah, live an' bigger'n Paul Bunyan."

"Aww, shit," David breathed.

Rez rumor, most especially Mug Row speculations, were not admissible in a court of law. But a big-mouthed witness like Irene Girard testifying that she saw Benny Peliquin prowling the murdered man's home playing peekaboo with the widow was.

Elliott sighed heavily. "You're right about the shit, boss. Benny's stepped into a big old pile of it this time."

"Elliott! What have I told you about graphics over the com line?"

Elliott was wounded. "Well, you started it!"

The offended dispatcher was gone. And there was no point trying to call him back. Elliott Raven could be a very pouty person.

TRACKER FOUND no dead man in Uncle Bert's bed, just rumpled sheets and blankets and more layers of dog hair. She didn't know yet if she was relieved. It had taken so much out of her to open the door and shine the spot beam inside that now she was shaking from head to toe. Leaning against the door-jamb, she took a moment to collect herself. Then she snatched up a soiled shirt from the bedroom floor and carried it outside.

Opening the passenger door, she shoved the shirt against Mushy's snout, giving the command "Hunt!" She'd just had time to toss the spotlight inside when Mushy took off like a bullet, going not for the woods behind the abandoned trailer, but down the weedy path that cut through the copse fronting Raspberry Road.

When she was six, her father had begun teaching her how to track. By the time she hit seven her father realized his daughter had an innate ability. He then turned her over to a young man then thought of as the best tracker on Red Cliff.

Benny Peliquin.

By the time she was ten years old, Benny declared his small pupil could track a partridge in flight. Which is how she'd earned her nickname, Tracker. She had never worked with a dog until she had res-cued Mushy and taught him to follow a scent. But unlike a bloodhound, Mushy didn't bay. Mushy ran like a silent streak. It was Tracker's job to keep up because Mushy wouldn't stop until he'd found what-ever it was he'd been instructed to sniff out.

Tracker's legs were pumping and her boots were leaving tracks in the muddy red clay as she crossed the width of Raspberry Road, then jumped the ditch and hit the woods on the other side. She couldn't see Mushy, but she could see the path he'd cut in the run through rain-sodden ferns and sapling brush. Tracker stayed on Mushy's trail even though when she reached the woods, there was only faint light filtering through the dense canopy and a mist floating above the spongy forest floor. As she moved through it, the mist parted, wafted away like a shy spirit. She'd barely run a quarter of a mile when she emptied her mind, allowing her inherent tracking ability to kick in. Benny called this *zoning*.

"Forget radios, TVs, any of that kinda crap, kiddo. None of that stuff's in the zone."

As a six-year-old, she'd been afraid. *"What's in that zone, Ben?"*

"Cool stuff, kid. Really cool stuff."

Benny had been right. In the zone she could hear her breathing, the thudding of her heart, and the blood coursing through her body. She was not hampered by physical things: the straining of her muscles, the branches that snagged at her clothing. Her hair, tied in a single braid, sailed behind her. In the zone, physical discomforts didn't exist. Then she heard Mushy barking. The realization that her dog had found something was enough to pull her out of the zone, and with such force that she stumbled and fell to her knees. Resting for a minute on all fours, she listened. Strange loud sounds echoed through the forest. But it was Mushy's frantic barking that pulled Tracker to her feet.

SHE DIDN'T HAVE a treat to give him as a reward. A pat and a "Good boy" would have to do. Mushy, standing on the very edge of the cliff overlooking Raspberry Bay, wasn't interested in any type of payment. The dog continued to howl at the huge flat-bottomed barge far below in the bay.

The salvage barge measured roughly eighty feet in length and twenty feet in width. The barge's crane was working, men running along the deck as the crane heaved a log out of the murky water. There was no mistaking the log for anything other than an old-growth white pine, for not since 1908 had there been any other log like it. These logs were the primary reason salvaging companies had marked the lake's bays off into a grid, had paid the state a king's ransom for the retrieval rights. The state of Wisconsin, not the Chippewa Nation, held the offshore rights along the reservation's coastline. This had the current Tribal Council firing reams of protests to the state's supreme court and barnstorming Washington, D.C., waving old treaties and Indian land-use agreements.

Yet here the salvagers were.

According to present state law, the salvagers

weren't operating illegally. Immorally, until the appeals were decided, most assuredly, but not illegally. And they were about a month too early. A risk foolhardy in the extreme, as there is nothing more dangerous than Lake Superior during early spring. Tracker also took note of the empty Zodiac moored just off the barge's stern. There was something puzzling about the inflatable, but she didn't have time to ponder what it might be as a man so tall that even at this distance he looked like a giant came out of the wheelhouse. It was apparent that he'd heard Mushy's barking even over the crane's noise. Holding a pair of binoculars to his eyes, he scanned the rim of the cliffs. Within seconds, she no longer heard the grinding noise of the crane, the muted voices of the men directing the newly upraised log. She no longer heard because she was feeling the big man's eyes boring into hers. Instinctively, her hand closed on Mushy's collar.

FREDDY HAROLD HAD always been big, so big that his mother had almost died during his birth. In fact, the delivery was so complicated that Freddy just barely escaped being born a total idiot. But he was slow, pathetically slow, unable to keep up with his classmates even though his teachers moved him right along with them through each grade. By the time he was eight, he had realized that he was different and that the other kids knew it and didn't like him for it. At eight, Freddy stopped being the play yard's gentle giant. The fear displayed by the other children pleased Freddy.

In the rough-and-tumble salvaging world, Freddy, in charge of security, was a highly valued employee. His present boss had repeatedly stressed that there were to be no witnesses to the current salvage operation, and Freddy had understood. However, the new job's location was so remote that the retrieval had gone along without a hitch. Freddy had been bored.

Until that old man had showed up.

Now, and on the same cliff top where the old man had appeared, was a little girl. Through the field glasses, Freddy honed in on her face. She was moving around a lot and twice he had to adjust the glasses in order to see her features clearly.

"You won't get away from Freddy," he muttered. Then with a shout, "I need the raft!"

TRYING TO PULL Mushy back from the edge was like trying to drag a moose. Barking threats at the men below, Mushy stood on his hind legs, back paws dug into the cliff's red soil with super dog purchase. Tracker pulled on his collar with all the strength she possessed. Finally she yelled, "End!" Mushy settled reluctantly, turning his face from her back toward the bay as she tugged him into the safety of cover and out of binocular range. Sweating profusely she knelt beside her dog, petting him, trying to force her mind back into the zone, a place where pure instinct was not only all-knowing, it was protective.

Tracker wanted to understand a lot of things at the moment, and that protective aspect would have been nice, too, but trying to launch herself into the zone never worked when her conscious mind was working overtime considering questions rising like bubbles. More pressing than any of the questions was her gut wisdom telling her to get the hell out of there.

Tracker went with her gut.

DAVID HAD JUST finished listening to Elliott's lengthy news item and was replacing the mike when through the cruiser's windshield, he spotted Tracker's truck. She had to be doing at least eighty.

"Holy shit!" he shouted.

And then his breath caught in his throat as her white truck skidded into the turn and only by sheer boneheaded luck did not flip sideways into the ditch. When the truck made it safely into the P.D. parking lot, he remembered to breathe. A second later he was cursing as he bolted out of the cruiser and ran for the footbridge to the police department's lot, lagging several paces behind Joey Du Bey.

SIX

TRACKER BAILED OUT of the truck, slamming the door and locking Mushy inside. Braid whipping behind her, legs pumping, boots thumping tarmac, she fixed her gaze on David, who was sprinting over the creek's footbridge. She didn't even notice Joey Du Bey until he was directly in front her, grabbing her arms. She tried to squirm away, tried breaking his hold. She couldn't see over Joey's shoulder, but she knew David was coming. She wanted to get to David. She needed to get to David. But Joey drew her in, held her hard against his side. The cause of the animosity between the two men was Joey Du Bey's determination to make Tracker his wife.

David was running up behind them. Joey could hear his approach and Tracker wriggled harder, trying to free herself. Joey tightened his hold and breathed into her ear, "I love you, Track."

Arriving on the scene and blowing like a horse, David yelled at Tracker: "Just what the hell were you doing?"

Tracker pushed against Joey, but Joey wasn't

ready to let go. David's fury and the volume of his voice increased tenfold. "Do you have any idea how fast you were going? You were on two wheels making that turn. You almost got yourself killed! I ought to write you up."

David's blast revived Tracker's temper and with one last shove she was able to disentangle herself. Finally facing David and feeling like a fool, she yelled right back. "You want to give me a ticket? Fine. Just don't forget to mention…" The toe of her boot made swift contact with David's shin.

"Je-sah!"

"…assaulting an officer." She rounded on Joey. "I have to report a missing person."

David was walking off the pain in his leg. Joey folded his arms across his chest, fighting the urge to grab her again. "Who's missing?" Joey asked.

Tracker answered in a burst of words. "My uncle Bert. I just came from his place. There isn't a sign of him or his wolf pack. I did find two lines of trout I figure to be about a week old. The fish were laid out on his table, like he was about to take care of them and then…didn't."

David came to stand directly behind her. "You do a search?"

Anger forgotten, Tracker spun on her heels to face him. "Yes. But not a big one. I sent Mushy to seek because that was quicker. Mushy went straight for the bay, David. Right for the cliffs. I didn't find

Uncle Bert, but you'll never guess what I did find.''
She went on to tell him.

"*Ho-le—*" David couldn't finish. "Track? Are
you sure?''

Hands on hips, she bent forward, yelling, "Do
you think I don't know a log recovery barge when
I see one?''

David exploded in kind. "Just calm down, will
ya? Your screaming is giving me a damn headache.
If you're right—"

"And I am!''

David's mouth curled in a snarl. Their eyes met
and held. David blinked first. He growled, "I've
gotta tell Frenchette.''

"I'll tell him myself.''

"Not you, me. He's not in any mood to have you
going at him like a fishwife.''

She opened her mouth to argue, but at that moment, from the corner of her eye, she saw the tribal
ambulance pulling out of the separate parking lot.
She watched the white van making the turn onto
Highway 13. The ambulance was not going in the
direction of the reservation hospital, nor was it using
its siren. Tracker's eyes cut back to David. "What's
going on over there?''

Their continuing war drifted into yet another
truce. For over two years now they were either
screaming at each other or uncomfortably polite.
Psychologists call this behavior sexual repression.

David and Tracker had come to know it simply as normal.

David took a deep breath, expelled it. "If you haven't heard the latest news, that makes you the one and only soul on Red Cliff." David shoved his hands deep into his jean pockets. "It's also the reason I was about to call you. I'm going to need your help."

"Oh, not again!"

STANDING BETWEEN David and Joey, Tracker felt like one of three naughty kids called into the principal's office. Seated in comfortable chairs facing the Tribal Chairman's solid oak desk were the BIA agent known as the Navajo, Sheriff Bothwell, and a blond deputy with eyes the color of blue ice. As David reported the barge sighting to Perry Frenchette, the Navajo, chewing on a thumbnail, watched the chairman's face mottle. Sheriff Bothwell, who didn't appear interested in what David was saying, propped his chin on his hands and offered her a smile and a quick wink. The blond deputy ignored her as he listened intently, hunching forward on the chair, arms braced on his knees. She knew the deputy was bursting with energy even though at the moment he was sitting perfectly still. His eyes watched all the players intently.

Perry Frenchette flew into a rage, hollering even before David was finished speaking. "Well, this is something I needed to hear today, of all days!'' David pressed his lips into a tight line as Frenchette rolled on. ''I'll personally look into the business in Raspberry Bay, but as for you, Lameraux, you're to concentrate on the killing. Or more to the point, finding Benny Peliquin—''

''Benny didn't do it,'' Tracker quickly interjected.

Perry Frenchette didn't cope well with being interrupted. Everyone working for him understood that whenever he launched himself into a tirade they were to wait humbly until he ran himself out. Before he'd fully recovered from her impertinence, Tracker spoke again.

''I've known Benny all my life. He's not a killer. You're after the wrong man.''

''My sister-in-law Thelma said—''

''I really don't care what Thelma said,'' Tracker replied, her inflection flat.

His face flushed with anger, the Tribal Chairman thundered, ''Young lady, this does not concern you.''

Tracker was not intimidated. ''Obviously Police Chief Lameraux thinks otherwise because he's asked me to join the search for Benny. But I'm afraid I can't help David just now. My uncle Bert is missing and finding him is my first priority.''

Frenchette's jaws bunched, relaxed, and bunched again as he literally chewed on his outrage. When he was finally able to trust himself to speak with any degree of composure, he said, "I understand family loyalty, but if my police chief feels he needs your aid, then as a full member of this community you are required to give it."

Tracker and the chairman made eye contact as the chairman's implication registered with every Indian in the room. Beside her, David and Joey shifted uncomfortably and sent her sideways glances. Feeling a strange undercurrent to the conversation and thoroughly interested because of it, Bothwell slouched, entwining the fingers of his hands and resting them atop the bulge of his belly. The Navajo seemed to be holding his breath as his eyes shifted between Tracker and Frenchette. Deputy Bjorke leaned even more forward and watched even more diligently as the silence extended, becoming a nonverbal confrontation between the chairman and the young woman.

Tracker's eyes didn't waver when she finally spoke directly to Frenchette: "As of this moment, you are responsible for my uncle." She turned away and had no more than closed the door behind her when Frenchette went off on David.

"You had no business hiring that woman without asking my permission first."

"Enlisting Tracker isn't anything I haven't done before," David said firmly. "If you expect us to find Benny, you *know* we need Tracker."

Frenchette glared, breathed hard through his nostrils, as he said, "Get out of here, Lameraux. I don't want to see your face again until Peliquin's in custody."

As David and Joey turned to go, Michael Bjorke leaped out of his chair, shadowing them. Not one of the three bothered closing the door.

Bothwell, a grin splitting his face, offered with a chuckle, "That boy of mine's a real go-getter. But he's a city boy. I think he's gonna have all he can do keepin' up with that little trackin' gal of yours. She's a hot little pepper, eh? If I was twenty years younger and fifty pounds lighter, I wouldn't mind trailin' through the woods after her myself. Think she'll really find Peliquin?"

Frenchette wasn't listening to the sheriff. His gaze lingered on the hallway just beyond the open door. Then he came back to himself with a snap. Lifting the receiver he said tersely, "If you'll excuse me, I have several calls to make."

"Uh-huh," Bothwell drawled. He shot a glance at the BIA agent. The Navajo was sitting back in his chair. Apparently the agent felt unaffected by Frenchette's acerbic dismissal. Bothwell's eyes shifted back to the chairman, who had finished dialing and was now standing with his back turned to the desk. Taking the hint, he slapped the chair's armrests and hoisted himself to his feet. "Well, guess I'll go get myself some breakfast."

BIA Agent Begay rose and followed a few paces

behind Bothwell, but the Navajo went no further than the edge of the doorframe, closing the door practically against Bothwell's well rounded hind end. The door was just clicking shut when Bothwell heard the Navajo ask, "Okay if I smoke?"

The diffident request was followed rapidly by a negative reply. The door now closed between him and the two men, Bothwell could hear their low-voiced exchange. Trouble was, he couldn't make out any of their words. He was tempted to press his ear against the solid wood and blatantly eavesdrop, but as his empty belly was screaming for attention, he didn't.

THE BLOND DEPUTY WAS really beginning to chap Tracker's lips. The four of them—David, Joey, Tracker, and Deputy Bjorke—were standing in the P.D. lot. David was trying to calm her down. Although she'd seemed in control during the meeting with Perry Frenchette, she'd been a breath away from exploding. Now that she was outside, a place relatively safe to explode while retaining some shred of dignity, Deputy Bjorke was talking about hunting Benny, just how they should go about catching a man that was closer to her than one of her own brothers. Bjorke went on babbling without any sign of let-up until Tracker had had more than enough.

Standing on tiptoe, Tracker got right in the deputy's face. "You're just all red-hot to have a manhunt, aren't you?'' she cried. "You must think that's really cool. Well, buster, let me tell you something. Manhunts are low-down, the nastiest business on earth. Outside of the police, you won't find any man on this entire rez ready to volunteer because hunting another human being just for the thrill is obscene. And one more thing, just while we're on the subject...I don't go in the woods with rookies.''

Michael's ice blue eyes locked on hers. Craning his head forward, his nose inches from hers, he said sharply, "This is *my* investigation. And you *will* go where I tell you to go, do what I tell you to do.''

Joey Du Bey intervened, wedging himself between Tracker and the deputy, forcing the latter to take a step back. "Don't talk to her like that. I mean it, man.''

Michael could tell that he did. The police chief, hands clenching and unclenching at his sides, looked as if he would happily join the fray. Two against one weren't Michael's favorite odds, yet he couldn't afford to back down. Speaking crisply, he said, "Let's all remember that we have a job to do and that like it or not, I am in charge. The three of you will cooperate or I will call in the feds.''

He was bluffing. David could smell the bluff all over him. Wisconsin, like four other states, was under the jurisdiction of Public Law 280, which in the fifties gave criminal and civil jurisdiction to state governments. Bayfield County police, even more than the Tribal Council, would fling themselves into hell's fires before relinquishing one shred of this power. But still, the deputy did have the authority to call in outside help if the locals refused to co-operate. And if the deputy did that, Frenchette would pop a major vessel.

David turned from Bjorke to Tracker. "We don't have time for a pissing contest, Track. The quicker we find Benny, the quicker we can start looking for your uncle Bert."

Tracker's eyes sparkled with contempt. David roughly grabbed her by the arm and pulled her off to the side for a private confab. "Listen to me, damn it," he whisper-shouted.

Tracker cut him off. "Even thinking I could come to you for help was a mistake."

David flinched. Then his pride rushed in and his spine straightened, his features hardening. "But old habits die kinda hard, don't they?"

They locked eyes, neither blinking. Before he said or did anything that would only make matters worse, David lifted his cap from his head, arm raked sweat off his brow. "We had one interesting call," he said. "I sent Mel to check it out. Mel radioed back that the tip was right. He found Benny's truck right where the tipster said it would be."

"Where?"

David told her. Tracker went a little pale. David shoved his face closer toward hers. "You know where he is, don'tcha?'' This wasn't a question. It was an accusation.

"Maybe," she breathed. His face was too close. She stepped back. Able to speak more clearly, she said, "But I do know something for sure." She glanced in the direction of Michael and Joey. Michael Bjorke dipped his head in an acknowledging bow. She didn't like the deputy, not at all. She turned back to David and said, "Baby-cakes over there is going to need a change of clothes. The bottoms of his shoes are too slick, and with all that stuff hanging off his belt, he jingles when he walks." That being the final thing she had to say, she began walking off in the direction of her truck.

David called after her. "Want us to meet at your cabin?"

She kept on walking, airily waving a hand over her shoulder: "Yeah, yeah. Whatever." Before opening the cab door, she yelled at Mushy, commanding him to move over into the passenger seat. The big dog reluctantly obeyed and she climbed in. Once she and Mushy were seated, she started the engine and pulled out without a backward glance at the three men watching her go.

AT HER CABIN, using the narrow mudroom entrance, Tracker and Mushy wedged themselves in through the door, the dog impatient to get to the water bowl, Tracker in a hurry to catch the steadily ringing telephone. Once they'd cleared the portal, Mushy was off in a run for the kitchen while Tracker raced for the living room. While lifting the receiver, she heard her father's angry voice.

"Where have you been? Did you know there's a stone killer running loose?"

Now the receiver was against her ear. "Dad—"

"Everybody's sayin' the killer's Benny. Don't that just beat the band? Just cause the boy was *poongin'* a married woman don't mean he killed her old man."

Tracker gasped loudly. "Are you saying Benny and Imogen Boiseneau…?"

Her father cut her off again. "Yeah, I'm sayin' it!" His voice lowered, became defensive. "But I'm not the only one. Folks have been talkin' about that for quite a while. It's sorta old news."

"Why didn't you tell me?"

Her father snorted derisively. "Oh, yeah, I'm gonna talk about who's poongin' who to my little girl."

Tracker bit her tongue. Her father would never change. It did her no good to argue that she was a fully grown woman. She could be facing fifty and her father would still refer to her as his little girl. She took a deep breath.

"Dad, I went over to check on Uncle Bert this morning."

"Yeah? Well, what's that old fart of a brother of mine up to?"

"That's what I'm trying to tell you. I think he's in trouble."

Tracker hurried to continue. George Charboneau did not interrupt so much as once. Uncle Bert was over ten years senior to her father. The age difference meant that they had never been close as brothers. But none of that made Uncle Bert any less of a brother.

When her father spoke, his anxiety was evident. "Okay, here's what we do," he said, taking charge. "You go on ahead an help out David so's Frenchette won't get his BVDs in a twist, an' me an' your brothers'll go lookin' for that old booger Bert. He's probably made himself a fish camp or somethin' and just forgot about those lines of trout rottin' in his trailer house. He's old, so that's something I wouldn't put past him. You don't worry your head one minute more about it. You just go on an' do what you gotta do."

"But if you need my help I—"

"Girl, I was walkin' these woods before you were even a twinkle! If I can't walk 'em now without you there to hold my hand, I might as well just go on ahead an' die."

Realizing she'd come perilously close to wounding her father's pride, Tracker readily surrendered. "I know that if anyone can find Uncle Bert, it's you.

What I meant was, if after I've helped David, Uncle Bert's still missing, I'll be ready to join the search.''

Placated, her father turned jocular. ''Well, okey-dokey. I'll keep that in mind, puddin'. I'm just glad to know that I raised you up right, taught you to appreciate that helpin' each other out is what families do. But I'll find Bert long before you ever find Benny, an' I got a twenty that says I will.''

''You're covered, Dad.'' She heard him chuckling as he put the phone down. Cradling the receiver, she was already running through the list of things that would need doing before David and his posse turned up.

Taking Mushy along was not an option. True, finding Benny would be faster with Mushy on the scent, but tracking a friend was bad enough. She simply refused to add the insult of using a dog. The issue of using Mushy was moot anyway if Benny's truck was close to the Sand River, as David had said. The country back in there was buck-wild. A dog would be more trouble than it was worth. David *had* been right about her knowing exactly where Benny was headed. Once, when she was a child, Benny had taken her to his secret place. It was possible he didn't remember having done it. On the other hand...

At any rate, his hiding out around the Sand meant that Benny would be zoning. He would have to. In that particular stretch of wild country, he would need all of his instincts and survival skills. The zone would ensure that his skills were flint-edged sharp. And while he was in that state, no one bogged in the twenty-first century would be able to touch him. David wasn't half as woodsy as he thought he was. He had never been taught to zone, most probably had no idea there was such a thing. Benny Peliquin had trusted only one other person with this special knowledge. Someone who'd faithfully sworn to keep the knowledge a secret.

Benny had passed on this special gift to her.

SEVEN

THERE WAS ALWAYS extra clothing stuffed inside the one and only locker in the P.D., but Michael Bjorke was proving hard to fit. Joey Du Bey came closest to his height, but Michael was more muscular than Joey, especially in the legs. As a result, Joey's available pair of jeans fit so snugly they looked as if they'd been painted on. The flannel shirt, light jacket, and well-worn boots were David's. The boots fit well enough, but the shirt and jacket were too big in the shoulders. While David and Joey concentrated on making Michael woods-ready, Elliott Raven made certain the four men going on the jaunt had an adequate food supply for three days.

Elliott Raven had known Tracker Charboneau before she was even born. He also knew how her father had taught her to think. For George Charboneau, his children's being able to survive in any and all situations was practically a religion. From the time his kids could walk and talk, George had drilled it into their heads that getting killed foolishly was, for a Charboneau, *the* one unforgivable sin. Therefore, if the four men preparing themselves to follow Tracker Charboneau ran out of food, they were simply doomed because Tracker would not share so much as a breath mint. Glad that he was old, that he was just the P.D. dispatcher, Elliott packed as much sugary and salty food as each backpack would hold. Sugar, provided by way of candy bars, would keep them going. Salty Ritz crackers would prevent their sweating out vital fluids. The protein in the string cheese and jerky would simply have to pass as a complete meal.

Melvin Paris would be the fourth man to be taking the hike through the North Woods. In his mid-twenties, Mel was short and solidly built, and because of an overabundance of French blood, his hair was chestnut colored and his eyes were bluish-grey. A police officer only in the spring and summer, Mel usually took orders well. He was an expert marksman, but he was most noted for being the departmental cold trail dog—the term for a hunting dog sent out before the rest of the pack. The type of game Mel Paris easily sniffed out was women, totally disarming them with an ingenuous smile and the cry of "Hey, you beautiful girl, you! Come on over here and give me a hug." A line that wouldn't work for any other man alive. Yet when Mel beckoned, women flocked. Far from being jealous, other men had learned to stay close, ready to snag—it was fervently hoped—any stray females Mel couldn't handle on his own. Not that there were many. Mel Paris was a notorious lover.

He was also a giggler.

As Elliott concentrated on the backpacks, Mel was giggling to himself, one gray blue eye sighting through the scope mounted on the bolt-action Winchester Model 70. There were no .308 shells in the magazine, which was lucky for Elliott, because Mel had the crosshairs trained on the back of the dispatcher's head. Elliott wasn't aware that his noggin was a target as he snapped the trail packs closed. Mel's index finger slowly squeezed, the subsequent click loud only to him.

Grinning like a naughty boy, Mel called out, "Hey, Elliott! Your head's a pulverized pumpkin, chum."

Elliott pivoted on the balls of his feet, eyes widening the instant he saw the weapon deliberately trained on him. For a moment all he could see was the weapon's dark mouth.

"Ho-wah!" Finally able to look away from the deadly barrel to the man behind the gun, Elliott felt his alarm turn to anger. "Damn you, Mel. Have you lost your rabbit-ass mind? Stop pointin' that thing at me."

Mel leisurely lowered the rifle, the grin he wore causing Elliott to think of a movie he'd seen once. A movie about a crazy gun-toting kid. Snippets of the film came to him, Technicolor scenes overlapping with reality, the young actor's face—indeed, his entire outlaw persona—blending into Mel's. The movie had been about Billy the Kid, and the way Mel Paris stood there holding the Winchester across his chest as he giggled made the creepy impression complete.

"It ain't loaded." Mel's shoulders shook as he snickered. "Your brains would be everywhere if it was."

Elliott's mouth was too dry to offer a reply. He was saved from any effort when David, glancing their way, said heatedly, "Mel, get the damn packs and wait for me in the Ram."

Obeying David's order meant that Mel came to stand toe-to-toe with the dispatcher. Rifle slung off his shoulder, Mel lifted all four backpacks off the counter. He chuckled at Elliott's bloodless face, then answered, "Yassuh, boss," to David.

Two seconds after Mel was out the door, Elliott turned on David. "That boy's crazy! Just pure crazy. You better watch him, David."

Petty squabbles among the troops were not something David was concerned with just at the moment. Benny Peliquin had been his friend for over half his life. David knew with certainty the type of weapon Benny would take into the bush, would be ready to use if he decided to make a stand. A scope-mounted Savage 110, .270 caliber. The same make Benny had once taught both Tracker and David how to treat with respect and use with lethal accuracy. Tracker still had her Savage. David had since changed—at departmental expense—to an AR15, the changeover coming during the year the budget had allowed the department's four 9mm Glocks. David had saved the cost of a fifth Glock by staying with his Smith & Weston .38 P/M. Glocks might be the sidearm of choice for most policemen, but David preferred the old Smith.

MUSHY FOLLOWED TRACKER as she emptied water buckets into his outside water trough. He stayed on her heels as she shouldered and carried the fifty-pound bag of dog food up the front porch steps, dropped it with relief, then used the knife sheathed on the left side of her jeans belt to cut a large X across the body of the bag. While she was away, the dog would have food and water. Should it rain, both the dog and his rations would be sheltered under the covered porch. Watching his mistress taking care of his water and food and then dragging his sleeping pallet out left Mushy in no doubt that his mistress was going somewhere without him. Mushy whimpered piteously.

Tracker ignored him.

She was still ignoring him minutes later inside the cabin as she hurriedly dressed in loose-fitting jeans, hiking boots, a long-sleeved white shirt, and a green baseball cap. Her camouflage backpack was prepared and waiting on the trestle table next to a spread-out Forestry Service map.

Her teeth scraped the corner of her mouth as she pored over the map. She liked to remember the Sand's wild country the way it had been before it had been clear-cut. In those long-gone days the Sand River area had had a wealth of secondary growth white pine and some impressive hardwoods. The loggers had been so thorough that they'd left the area devastated. She'd deliberately avoided that area until last year, when she'd had to go in there after a lost teenager. It hadn't come as any surprise that the recovering landscape was now a nearly impenetrable thicket of close-standing trees no bigger around than her arm. All in all, a bad place for anyone to be hunting. What made the Sand irresistible to a novice hunter was that deer favored the place. The kid had been easy to find because he desperately wanted to be found and because he'd walked primarily in circles. That had made her job simple without her having to walk too far in.

Benny wouldn't be easy to locate. He wasn't afraid or desperate. And he certainly didn't want the police to find him.

A clock ticked away inside her head as she studied the map, the clock representing her uncle's life. Despite her father's assurances, he would need her quite badly if he still hadn't managed to locate Uncle Bert by the end of the day. Which meant that if

Uncle Bert was still alive, she would have to join that search no later than tomorrow. She put her mind so wholly to the task of memorizing the map that she didn't hear, until Mushy began to bark, the vehicle pulling into the drive. Tracker shoved the map aside, grabbed up the backpack, then raced Mushy to the front door.

MICHAEL SAT FORWARD in the front seat of the extended cab, staring through the windshield as Tracker, standing on the lip of the front porch, repeatedly ordered a huge dog to stay. The dog wasn't inclined to comply. Finally, backpack slung over one shoulder, she came down the steps. Michael then watched her through the side mirror as she tossed her pack into the truck bed with the others. David, hands resting on the steering wheel of the idling rust-red 4 X 4, was also watching her, eyes raised to the rearview mirror. Directly behind them, Mel popped open the cab's back door and leaned out. "Hey, Track! Get on in here, girl, an' give me a hug!"

Tracker climbed in, settling next to Mel on the back bench. Seated on the other side, Joey watched her, his lips thinning as Mel and Tracker hugged. Mel, feeling the heat of Joey's jealousy building, giggled.

"Track!" David said abruptly. "Didn't you kinda forget your rifle?"

Tracker extricated herself from Mel, took a rapid scan of the armory of the four men. She answered his question with another. "Wouldn't that be over-kill?"

David fumed silently as she directed him down Allen Road, had him turn on County K and then take a left on Highway 13. Quickly realizing where she was directing him, he yelped, "Hey! I hope you're not taking us where I think you are."

Tracker squirmed on the crowded back bench, pushing off Mel's attempt at another cuddle. "Yes, I am."

David, continually checking the rearview mirror, was sorely tempted to reach back and just pop Mel. Michael, taking mental notes, felt the tension level in the truck steadily rising. The police chief and Du Bey maintained a stony silence, both of them acutely aware of Tracker's whispered *don't*s and Mel's in-ane giggling. It came as a relief for everyone, save Mel, when the sign for Big Sand Bay Road came into view. David slowed the truck, pausing on the verge of what was little better than a dirt path.

Big Sand Bay Road was widely known as a haz-ard. In a wet spring, such as this one, Big Sand Bay Road became a plethora of potholes, some so large they were capable of swallowing a tank. It was only in the driest stretch of summer that the road received a grading, the potholes a gravel backfill. And even then the road was barely usable.

"Damn it, Track!" David yelled at full volume. "This truck's almost new. You gonna foot the bill if the axle snaps?"

"No."

"Then think of something else."

"I would," she said, "if we had time. We don't. So it's follow the Big Sand Bay, Jeeves, and don't spare the horses."

"Jeeves," Mel snickered, then snorted. "You're a funny girl, you know that, Track? An' ya give great hug. Hey! I gotta idea. Why don't you marry me?"

"Mel!" David and Joey shouted.

ALONG BIG SAND Bay Road, impressive pines gave way to walls of stalk-thin poplars, tag alders, birches, and waist-high canary grass. The truck was brutally jostled from one pothole to the next, making Michael feel as if he were riding a mechanical bull. After yet another slam to the undercarriage, he glanced at David. "Was there a big fire back here?"

"Nah," David said. His hands were locked on the steering wheel as he hunched forward, his eyes trained on the rutted and steadily narrowing road. "About fifteen years or so ago, they clear-cut all the way down to the ground and then this mess of sun worshipers grew up."

Michael looked out the side window again. "Looks rough."

"It is," David snorted. "Last year a first-time deer hunter, a sixteen-year-old, thought he could get away with doing something us oldsters wouldn't even try. Anyway, three days later his mama called the station, crying for her baby. As soon as she told me where he went, I knew we'd have to go in for the little shit. Luckily for us, Tracker was able to find him."

Michael looked again at the scenery, awed by the maze of trees. He half turned, looking at her over his shoulder. "You're really that good?"

She averted her eyes, then said, "Yes, I am." Michael continued to watch her as she snapped at David, "But if you'll recall, I didn't exactly find that kid all by myself."

Michael turned forward, looking at the police chief, waiting for him to speak. David said nothing, keeping his eyes trained forward. Tracker was right, of course. Although at this juncture he didn't feel inclined to acknowledge the fact that she hadn't headed the search party.

Benny Peliquin had.

Benny knew this region of sapling forest, shifting sand cliffs, and meandering river almost as well as he knew the back of his own hand. Yet Tracker had been the one who'd found the kid's trail, and then a short time later, the kid. She'd said it was an easy find because the kid had been so scared. Her pointed reminder was meant to convey that Benny wouldn't be afraid, that locating him wouldn't be an easy twenty-minute walk into the back of the beyond. David chose not to rise to the bait. Arguing would defeat his purpose, for truth be told, Tracker was his only hope of finding Benny.

Again staring out the window, Tracker thought about Benny's truck, where it had been found abandoned on County K at Bench Mark 900. His leaving his truck there was just a bit too obvious for two reasons. For one, leaving his truck parked on the side of a regularly used road meant that it would be seen. And for the second, if Benny really wanted to hide from the law, he had plenty of places to stash the truck, knowing it wouldn't be found for weeks. As small as the reservation was, without this clue as to where to start looking for him, she would have been stumbling blindly around for God knew how long. She hadn't even thought of Sand River until David had told her precisely where they had found Benny's truck.

David had expected her to begin the search at Bench Mark 900. Had she done that, she could easily have picked up Benny's trail along the creek that fed into the Sand River. But because she had an idea of his actual direction, she'd bullied David into taking Big Sand Bay Road. This way, she would be coming in on Benny from behind. For now, she began to think of ways to shake off her police escort.

She was still mulling this over when the truck

came to a complete stop. Realizing they'd arrived at the end of Big Sand Bay Road, she popped open the door and jumped out, running to the flatbed to retrieve her backpack. She was already slipping her arms through the shoulder straps when the others joined her. The four men were talking; Tracker heard their voices, but their words skimmed right past her. They were still talking when she set off, working to put distance between herself and them. Once she was inside the blind of thin trees, she couldn't see them, but she could clearly hear the Bayfield deputy swearing a blue streak.

Even for a seasoned woodsman the trek was a nasty slog. For a rookie it had to be hell, especially as swarms of bloodthirsty insects eagerly made everything twice as bad. But the deputy's yelps disturbed the stillness. Livid, she turned and backtracked.

TIPPING HER HEAD BACK against her shoulders erased the shadow caused by the bill of her baseball cap. David had a clear view of her upturned face as she spoke in a low-voiced growl. "If *you* can't keep him quiet, give me your pistol."

His tongue protruding slightly between his lips, David unsuccessfully fought a smile. He looked away for a second, then back down to Tracker. "Don'tcha think shooting at him would be louder than his bitchin'?"

"Maybe," she said. "But Benny might mistake the shots for a poacher."

David slapped the insect stinging the side of his neck, looked at his hand, flicked the dead creature away. "Tell you what, I'll bathe all us manly guys in repellent and then we won't bother you with our complaints."

"It's not perfumed, is it?"

David looked irritated. "No. It's fragrance-free for sensitive skin."

Tracker rolled her eyes, not amused. "I'm going on up ahead. You'll be all right as long as you keep heading west. I'll always know exactly where you are. I won't lose you."

David craned forward, said just loud enough for her to hear, "Correct me if I'm wrong, but isn't that the same thing you promised a couple of years ago?"

Blood rushed to her cheeks. Then her eyes turned hard and she squared her shoulders and walked away. Just a few steps further into the brush, Tracker vanished.

HEADING EAST and now a good half a mile away from the men, she was zoning, any and all disruptive thoughts of David banished. Deep in the zone she was able to glide through the worst of the dense brush and tag alders. The shore of the Sand River was firm enough to jog along as she followed the circuitous river in its determined course to the big lake. An hour later, she veered off, plowing straight up a steep incline, breaking through the barrier of canary grass, where she was once again immersed in stands of immature poplar, birch, and tag alders growing so close together that more often than not she literally had to squeeze herself between them. Sweat poured down her face into her eyes. Tracker felt no discomfort as she plodded steadily onward.

EVERY PARTICLE OF her was wholly submerged in her surroundings. She listened to birds sing and recognized each species by its song, heard the partridges thumping loudly against hollow deadfall and the rustling of unseen tiny mammals skittering around her crouched form. Peering through the soughing grasses, she also heard the crackle of a branch and knew by the sound that a velvet-bumped buck was very close, that it was pausing to test the air. She felt the buck's wariness, then felt it relax.

Time had no meaning in the zone. For Tracker, since the buck's presence had been noted and the deer had moved off, only one or two minutes had gone by. Actually, it had been closer to thirty when her heightened senses detected the movement of a black bear sow and cub. Both came lumbering close to where she sat, arms wrapped around her knees, boots planted so firmly that they were buried deep in the red sandy soil. Both mother bear and cub ambled by without noticing the human so close to them that Tracker could have reached out and touched one or the other.

More time passed, the shadows shifting from those of mid-morning to those of high noon. Tracker had not moved so much as a fraction of an inch, yet she felt no cramping of muscles, no needs of any kind. Nor was she concerned that David and the others might catch up with her, blunder into the little trap she'd set for Benny. She'd sent David west, straight into the worst of the region. He and his crew would hike up hills and down gullies believing all the while that she was just a few yards ahead, never once suspecting that she was keeping watch over a stretch of wild rice. The tall rice stalks protruding above a field of water were courtesy of a band of beavers, the industrious creatures having dammed up this section of the Sand River, inadvertently creating a rice bed known to no one else on the reservation.

Except Benny.

He'd brought her to this place only once, when she was a child. For that one season, they'd been a ricing team, Benny poling the canoe through the choke of plants while Tracker knelt at the front, using white cedar sticks to knock the rice grains into the boat. The rice from this field had to be the best she'd ever tasted. Her father thought the same thing. He'd also wanted to know just where the rice had come from. Tracker remained silent, keeping Benny's secret even though she was disappointed when Benny didn't ask her to rice with him the following season or the next. After that, and until today, she had forgotten.

Eventually something outside the realm of commonplace rustling and twittering touched her mind. The muted sounds were unhurried. More than that, they were controlled. Tracker decided to wait a bit, to allow Benny more time. He was a lot older now than when he'd taught her the ways of the woods, the pathway into the zone.

He'd also taught her something else. That the older a person grew, the harder it was to remain in the zone for any length of time. The mind was willing, but older bodies couldn't take the strain. She continued to wait even when a passing breeze brought to her a whiff of thin smoke. Tracker grinned. Benny was so cool. Exhausted as he had to be, he wasn't sloppy. In making a fire he'd gone for the wood on the beaver lodge, wood stripped of bark and aged—the kind of wood that would produce only the barest trace of smoke. Even now the smoke was so faint that if she hadn't been in the zone, she wouldn't have smelled it at all. Nor would she have caught the scent of burning paper, the label on the can he'd opened and set in the fire. Inhaling deeply she recognized his favorite meal.

Spaghetti-O's.

Tracker stood for a moment while her body adjusted itself. The slowdown of her heartbeat, the near shutdown of blood flow to the extremities was one of the reasons zoning for a long time could be so dangerous, why older bodies rebelled against such prolonged mental freedom. And as she slowly withdrew from the zone, she felt the strain the sustained crouch had placed on her knees, ankles, and feet. As her heart rate returned to normal every vein in her legs reacted to the sudden whoosh of blood, sending back the sensation she was being stung by hundreds of wasps. She winced, lifting one numb foot, then the other, and gingerly setting them down.

It was damn near impossible to remain in shape during the long winters. This past winter her cousin Patti had decided that every Monday night would be fitness training in Patti's basement. Well, that hadn't worked, mainly because four other cousins were included and Monday nights quickly became a six-woman party; the one nod to fitness was the Red Cliff stair-climbing exercise. This wasn't a machine, but a race up the basement stairs, through the kitchen (pausing just long enough to grab a buffalo wing and a can of Miller Lite), out onto the back porch, down those stairs, around the house, and back down into the basement, with a stop to dump chicken bones and emptied beer cans into the trash barrel. Then the entire process was repeated. Thanks to the Monday night exercise sessions at cousin

Patti's, Tracker was coming out of the previous winter five pounds heavier.

And at this moment, she was feeling every one of them.

EIGHT

HUNKERING WITH his left haunch on his ankle, right leg slightly extended, Benny fed bleached sticks to eager flames. Hearing a steady movement, he dropped the sticks and slid his arms between his legs, his hands touching the rifle lying beneath him. He listened keenly, knowing after a space of seconds that he was listening to an Indian. Indians habitually walk toe-in and in a winding pattern. Non-Indians walk like ducks and dead-on straight, trampling everything with a *splat-splat* stride. The Indian he was listening to sounded very light. Benny relaxed, went back to tending the fire.

A minute passed. Then from the corner of his eye he watched Tracker approach, coming in slowly, her hands on top of her baseball-capped head, fingers entwined. She stopped about a half dozen feet away. Benny looked up from the fire and they stared at each other in an uncomfortable silence.

Finally Benny spoke. "What you doin', girl?"

Hands remaining on top of her head, Tracker shrugged her shoulders. "Same as you, I guess. Just taking a walk in the woods. Nice day for it. Biting flies aren't too bad and the sun's not too hot. Yep, it's a pretty good day for a walk."

"Huh," he grunted, looking away, back at the fire. Lip pointing to the blackened can sitting amid the flames he said, "Think maybe all your walking made you hungry?"

"I could eat," she returned.

"Come on in, then."

As she came forward, Tracker unlocked her hands, arms dropping to her sides. Entering the makeshift camp she paused, removed her backpack, dropped it close to Benny, and made her way to the other side of the fire. The backpack had landed with a whoosh, raising red dust. Benny, while eyeing the bag, fanned the dust away from his face. Squinting, he looked at the backpack. One old friend suspecting another was embarrassing. Depositing the backpack within his easy reach was Tracker's way of giving consent to his searching through the contents.

Benny didn't bother. Instead, he nodded his approval and said, "You've always been a good kid, Track." His voice, still low, took on a dejected tone. "I'm just sorry it was you they sent for me."

"No, you're not." Because her legs still hurt, she crossed them, then leaned forward. "You wanted me to come. That's why you sent the message. You know the message I mean. The way you left your truck."

Benny tried to look innocent. The attempt failed miserably. Snickering, he said, "Okay, truth is, I was hoping you'd be just a little slower on the up-take." His lopsided grin slowly faded, became a grim line. He looked out over the stretch of water and the glut of bright green rice. "We once had ourselves a good old time in this place, eh?"

"The best," she sadly agreed.

He looked away, sighed heavily, and then went quiet. Tracker waited. Eventually he asked, "How far back you leave David?"

Tracker's answer was a toothy smile.

Benny's taut features eased. Seconds later, as realization dawned, he gasped, "Where the hell'd you send him?"

"West."

Benny's face twisted with both amusement and distaste. "Oh, man! Track, that's just pure mean. The only thing meaner would be losing him in Bibbon Swamp."

"I considered it." She laughed.

"I bet you did," he said, laughing with her.

CANNED SPAGHETTI always tastes best when cooked in an open fire and singed inside the can until the normally runny ketchup sauce is sludge thick. Sitting side by side, Tracker and Benny ate out of the can he held from the bottom, his hand protected by a leather glove. They had been sharing field lunches since she'd been six, and had the dipping process down pat, Tracker's spoon going in first, gentleman Benny's second. Benny always packed Spaghetti-O's because the little rings of pasta were easier to eat than the stringy stuff. Between bites, they talked.

"I didn't kill that asshole."

"I know."

Benny pulled his head back. "Oh yeah?"

Tracker spooned more food into her mouth. Benny looked down at the can. Only a little bit left. He went for it, his metal spoon clanking against the sides of the can. Tracker licked the remaining traces of sauce off her spoon, then tossed it inside her opened pack.

Sitting back, resting on her elbows, she said, "David said Jud was shot with a pistol. I know you have an old .38. I also know it hasn't worked in years."

"Maybe I fixed it."

"Huh," she snorted. "Just like you fixed that old Skidoo sled."

Benny, his mouth full, became defensive. "Hey! Snow machines are tricky. Ya gotta work on 'em real careful."

"But not so carefully the thing becomes obsolete and the manufacturer stops making the parts."

Benny chuckled. "So I was a little too careful about the sled. That don't mean nothing about my pistol."

She tipped her head back, looking up at the sky. Slate gray clouds were gathering. It would begin raining within a few hours. Worrying now about David being lost and caught out in a storm, Tracker sat up, came hurriedly to the point. "Ben, I know about you and Imogen."

Benny blinked his eyes, trying the innocent bit again. He was stalling. Ordinarily she would have played along, but because of David and her continued sense of urgency about Uncle Bert, Benny's tactics were making her angry. "I've also heard stories that Jud didn't always play nice with Imogen. My question is, did he start getting rough before or after he found out you were poongin' her?"

"Hey!" he yelped. He shot her a look of fury. "Track, I won't let even you talk about her like that."

Tracker went on regardless. "What happened, Ben? Did Jud finally beat her so badly that she popped him? If that's true, then Imogen can plead self-defense. Everybody on Red Cliff will back her up, most especially David. She won't even see the inside of a jail, never mind go to prison. But you…" She removed her cap, wiped her forehead, replaced the cap. "If you try to take the blame for her…" Tracker paused meaningfully. "Ben, they'll put you under the damn prison."

The entire time she was speaking, Benny used his spoon to dig a hole in the soft earth between his booted feet. He set the emptied can inside the hole, covered it over, patted down the soil. "Seems to me this is a fine old case of the pot callin' the kettle." He emitted a humorless chuckle, looked her hard in the eyes. "You've never listened to me when it came to your love life, so why the hell should I listen to you about mine?"

Tracker tapped her fingertips against her chest as her voice got louder. "Because unlike you, *I'm* not willing to throw my life away on someone else. I—"

"Live with a dog," he cut in, his tone dull, weary. "You take care of that ugly hound when you should have a husband and real children." He locked her eyes with his. "Ya ain't exactly a spring chicken, ya know. You're gonna wake up one mornin' and it's all gonna be gone, too late to be a wife, way too late to be a mama. Whatcha gonna do then, Track?"

Tracker's eyes narrowed. She was too angry to answer.

Benny shook a finger westward, saying, "Out there somewhere—if he hasn't fallen off a cliff and killed himself—is the man you were meant to marry. When something's meant, there just ain't no use tryin' to fight it. An' that's how it is with me an' Imogen. The very same."

Tracker's face was bloodless, her voice a croak. "Yeah, you're right. It is the same. Imogen's suckered you the same way David suckered me. It's time we both faced it. The great loves of our lives only used us for all we were worth.''

Benny jumped to his feet, hollering at her. "If you're just gonna think that kinda shit, I ain't gonna bother to talk to you no more.'' In a sulk Benny picked up his pack and rifle. "I think maybe I'm gonna find David, do my surrenderin' to him.''

THEY HIKED FOR an hour without speaking. She'd never walked for so long and through such dense growth without the benefit of zoning. She couldn't say she appreciated the drudgery au naturel, but as the man who'd taught her to zone was technically her prisoner, she had to stay in the moment. Even if that moment entailed sweating buckets, suffering bug bites, and feeling the ache and strain in every one of her muscles. At some point she decided to make an attempt at conversation. Benny, his feelings still hurt, didn't respond. At least until she poured out her concerns for her uncle, and in doing so, off-handedly mentioned the recovery barge in Raspberry Bay.

Benny came to a stop and asked her to begin again, to tell him everything as it had happened. Tracker sighed wearily. Her pack felt too heavy and her entire body was clammy with sweat. She did as he'd asked, however, telling him all about Uncle

Bert's trailer and his disappearance, ending with the discovery of the barge.

"An' it was working?"

"Yeah," she panted, mouth dry, tongue thick.

Benny mulled, scratching the back of his head. "That just ain't right, Track."

She filled her lungs with air, released it slowly through her nose. "Perry Frenchette said the salvagers were too early, but he—"

"No!" Benny shouted. He stepped nearer, agitated. "Look, I know I haven't been working the boats for about a week, but that don't mean a whole lot in the salvaging business. For one thing, any operation like that has to have divers come in first. Finding sunken logs ain't the problem, it's checking out the markings. The divers have gotta do that because if they see U.S. marks, those logs can't be brought up."

"I don't understand," she said, shaking her head.

Benny launched into a lengthy explanation.

"Okay, this is how it went back in the olden days when there was plenty of ancient white pines and the harvesting was being done by individual logging operations. Everybody's logs always got mixed up during the float down to the lake, so to keep ownership straight, before a log was skidded, sledgehammers with different marks on the heads were used to hammer the rightful owner's imprint into the log. It was kinda like a brand but deeper, and every owner's symbol was registered. The symbol marking the logs that went to the entire Chippewa Nation was U.S.

"The way the state courts have decided the recovery rights is that any log carrying a defunct logging company mark is up for salvaging grabs, *but*"—he emphasized the word—"any log with the U.S. mark still belongs to us Shinabes. Which means salvagers have gotta send in the divers first to make damn sure whatever's down there is something they can keep. Otherwise, all they're doin' is workin' for us. And at their expense."

Benny shoved his hands deeply into his pockets, rocked back on his heels. "I know you don't know diddly about boats, but take it from me, barges are clumsy beasts. This early in the season, a good barge captain ain't gonna take it on the lake just for grins. And a barge is too big to hide even on the Big Lake. It also makes a hell of a noise. So now you answer me this question: How do you suppose diving teams worked Raspberry Bay long enough to check all that out and then give the all clear for the barge to come cutting through our fishing waters without even one fisherman ever noticing?"

That was a long question. And a very good one. After a considerable think, Tracker admitted she had no answer.

Benny nodded. "That's why there's something real wrong with everything you just told me."

They began walking again; this time Tracker was the uncommunicative one. She heard Benny's voice, but she wasn't listening to his words. She kept her head down as she tagged after him, concentrated on placing her feet inside Benny's prints—a little game he'd taught her when instructing her in the ways of the woods. While other little girls were making a game of being careful not to "step on a crack, break your mama's back," Tracker was being taught to stretch her little legs to match his stride, walk lightly and place her foot inside the print of his boot. In essence, Benny had been teaching her how to be invisible, to fool anyone following them into believing he was following one person, not two. She'd fallen back into the old game so completely that she stepped on the back of his boots when he stopped suddenly, looking down at the obvious signs. She'd moved back a safe distance when he rounded on her.

"Hey! You didn't say nothin' about David havin' a Chamook with him."

Now able to see the signs Benny saw, Tracker did a quick study of the four separate courses left through the tangle of growth, her gaze settling on the one that followed too straight a route. "That's the Bayfield deputy."

Offended, Benny said peevishly, "Ole Dave sure was quick to get the sheriff on to me."

She hated having to come to David's defense. "This is his first murder case, Ben. What was he suppose to do? Wait for his prime suspect to just wander on in?''

''It's what Elmer would have done.''

Benny was referring to Elmer Crane, a man so inattentive to duty that for years Red Cliff for all intents and purposes didn't really have a police chief. Eventually Elmer's lackluster policing methods rubbed the locals' nerves raw. One of the campaigning promises made by Perry Frenchette was that if he was elected Tribal Chairman, easygoing Elmer would be out. That promise alone won him the election. During his first week as chairman, Perry appointed David the new police chief.

Benny worked up more of a temper about the Bayfield deputy. ''This changes everything, Track. I was gonna do this peaceable, but now David can just keep on lookin' for me until one of us is too old to wiggle. An' as for you—''

Tracker raised a silencing hand. ''If you think I'm going to wrestle you to the ground and handcuff you, you're out of your mind. For one thing, I don't have any handcuffs. For another, I think I need you to stay free.''

Benny raised a suspicious brow. ''What are you gettin' at, girl?''

''How long do you think it would take you to get back to where you left your truck?''

Benny's eyes flared. ''Shit! All the way back there?''

"Yeah."

He looked into the distance, heaving a full sigh. "Couple of hours. But that would mean hauling some serious ass."

"Then haul away."

Benny was incredulous. "You're really cuttin' me loose?"

"On your promise you'll stay low until I come back to get you."

Benny's brain was changing gears. She could almost hear the grinding. "My truck—"

"It's not there." She quickly put the brake on that hope. "It's been impounded."

Benny looked sourly at her. "I might decide to play along with whatever it is you've got cooking. But what are you going to say to David?"

"As little as possible."

Despite himself, Benny chuckled. "Same as always, eh?"

"SON OF A BITCH!" Michael Bjorke roared.

"Don't move," David said, working to keep his tone calmer than he felt. He showed the palms of his hands, pressing them against the air. "You've walked into a quick bog. We can get you out, but you've got to be as still as possible."

"Jesus, Mary, and Joseph," Joey breathed, watching the watery ground rising around the deputy. "He's sinking kinda fast."

The bog was climbing up the deputy's legs, reaching the knees, oozing steadily upward. Watching the bog's deadly progress, Mel commenced to giggle uncontrollably. Hurriedly shrugging off his backpack, David spoke sharply to his officer. "Mel! You got any rope in your pack?"

"Yeah, boss."

"Well, get it out!"

WHEN TRACKER eventually found them, all four men were sitting on a sandy incline looking as if they'd just barely survived a war. David, arms draped over his raised knees, was wearing his baseball cap backwards, his fully exposed face shiny with sweat. Every bit of his clothing was clinging to him like an outer layer of filth. His eyes nailed her as she slid down the incline on the sides of her feet, came to a stop. Standing over him, she provided some shade from the sun, which was still managing to break through the thickening clouds.

"Had some trouble, huh?"

"You could say that," he answered tersely. His eyes flickered toward his equally filthy cohorts, then back to her. "Our Bayfield boy walked into a boggy patch. Took every bit of strength we had to pull him out." David mimicked a Cuban accent. "So, Lucy, how was your day?"

Tracker fought off the urge to smile. David imitated Ricky Ricardo whenever he was positive she'd been up to something. Before she could respond, Joey rose to his feet, came to stand beside her.

"Hey, Track? You pick up any sign of Ben?"

"Yeah."

Joey became impatient, snapping, "Where?"

"Up a way. But I lost him again." Tipping her head back, she looked up at the sky. "Figured I'd better quit and find you guys. It's gonna rain. This would be a bad place to wait out a storm."

Joey looked up at the building sky as if noticing it for the first time and said under his breath, "Ho-le."

She felt David's stare as she and Joey watched the clouds swirl, swallow the sun whole. The entire sky went black, and the air was so thick with building humidity it was well nigh chewable. Forcing herself to meet David's eyes, she said, "We're gonna have to hustle if we're gonna get Golden Boy to safer ground."

"If you're referring to me," Michael said snidely, "I can take anything you or Mother Nature can dish out."

Tracker looked across to the deputy. Exasperated, she said, "Yeah? Looks to me like *Mama* almost sucked you down like a piece of candy."

Half reclining against the sandy knoll, Mel didn't giggle. He fell against his back and bayed.

NINE

IT WAS BEGINNING to rain, droplets hitting the dingy gray asphalt and marking the parking lot with quarter-sized splotches. Normal Indians never run in the rain, but Perry Frenchette wasn't a normal Indian. During his dash the low-hanging heavens opened up and the rains began in earnest. Cussing under his breath he shielded his head with his briefcase and sprinted. Reaching his car he climbed inside, slamming the door. The car started up, the windshield wipers doing what they could to sluice fan-shaped openings in the downpour.

Barely three minutes later, the Tribal Chairman left his car parked in the shelter of the hospital's breezeway and barreled through the glass double doors into the lobby. A good number of people were sitting on the couches and chairs, most of them knowing enough to bring a book to read while enduring a lengthy wait. A crowd of children filled the hospital playroom. Not only could he see them through the glass walls, he could hear their squeals and one or two arguments over the toys. He contin-

ued on, passing the reception desk. Two reception-
ists who knew from past experience that it was use-
less to try to slow him up glanced meaningfully at
each other, rolling their eyes. He hung a quick right
after the reception counter, his determined step silent
along the carpeted hallway. Five patients dressed in
disposable paper gowns sat uncomfortably in plastic
chairs as they awaited their turn at being X-rayed.
One or two of the men nodded as their chairman
steamed on by. The office he wanted was at the far
end of the corridor. Reaching the door, he opened it
without bothering to knock.

Wanda DuPree glared at him, stepping back from
the man seated in a padded swivel chair and closing
a patient file folder. Perry, as well as everyone else
on the rez, knew that Wanda and her husband were
having their troubles. Ralph DuPree was the only
mechanic on Red Cliff, and a shade tree mechanic
at that. Ralph was a jury-rig genius, a gift he called
Injun-nuity. Ralph needed to be a genius in order to
keep Indian cars running decades beyond the auto-
motive manufacturer's suggested life expectancy.
Wanda was rumored to have set her sights a tad
higher, in fact on the man now peering myopically
at the Tribal Chairman.

Frenchette said to the seated doctor, "We've gotta
talk."

"I don't suppose you could wait five minutes?"
"No."

With a sigh, Ricky gave Wanda a dismissive wave. As she walked by, the overhead lights reflected off the back of her nylon skirt. Frenchette couldn't help but notice that beneath the uniform Wanda wasn't wearing a slip. What he did see was a garter belt holding up the pair of white stockings encasing her long, slender legs. Garter belts were such a turn-on. In Perry's opinion, the guy responsible for the invention of pantyhose should be hunted down and drawn and quartered.

Several times.

On her exit, Wanda closed the door noiselessly behind her. Frenchette moved to the vacant chair and sat down. Coming straight to the point, he said flatly, "I'm having a real problem with that damn Navajo."

Resting his chin in his palm, Doc Ricky found himself held captive in the throes of one of Perry Frenchette's diatribes. This had been going on for weeks. Doc Ricky was reaching the end of his tether. Then, in the midst of the discourse, Frenchette said something that caused Ricky to sit up and take full notice. Half an hour later, Perry had blown himself out. Feeling better, he left. Doc Ricky picked up the telephone. It was answered on the third ring.

"Wanda? Come back to my office, would you, please?"

THE RAINS SLAMMED the truck relentlessly as David negotiated the total washout of Big Sand Bay Road. The truck fishtailed just after barely clearing what had once been an annoying chuckhole but was now, under the steady watery assault, an arroyo. They hadn't managed to reach the shelter of the truck before the rains hit, so as a consequence, everyone was soaked to the bone. They were also shivering because the cab's heater wasn't doing all that much. The windshield, because of the foggy breath created by five hyperventilating humans, steamed over again and again. David used his hand to swipe an open space, then went back to white-knuckling the steering wheel.

As bad as the storm was becoming, David wasn't worried about Benny being caught out in it. A true jack pine savage, Benny was able to go deep in the woods equipped with only a knife and a length of picture wire and come out some weeks later healthier than when he'd gone in. Nope, a spot of rain wouldn't give Benny Peliquin anything worse than a needed bath. Just at this moment David was more concerned about himself, for not only was he responsible for the well-being of the nearly new tribal vehicle, there were four lives to consider. If he somehow got the three guys killed, sooner or later he'd be absolved of that tiny faux pas, but the death or injury of Tracker would absolutely never be forgiven. All things considered, David began to feel that his suspect was getting the better end of this particular deal, and under his breath David cussed Benny Peliquin.

David didn't know a relieved breath until he pulled into the driveway fronting Tracker's cabin.

He yelled to her as she cracked open the door, pushing hard against the wind and driving rain. "As soon as this mess clears out, we're making another try for Ben."

Tracker nodded and jumped out. The wind caught the door, closing it so hard the truck rocked. Tracker bent into the wind, struggling forward toward the safety of her cabin. On the porch Mushy was barking at the truck. Finally realizing that the intruder was his mistress, the big dog bolted to meet her halfway. A minute later the two of them were safely inside the warm dry cabin, Tracker more than happy to dump her heavy backpack. It fell to the floor behind her ankles, and as rainwater trickled down her face, she went to peer through the window, watching the headlights as the Dodge Ram steadily reversed out of the drive. As soon as the truck's lights were aimed down Little Sand Bay Road, she hurried away from the window, creating a trail of muddy boot prints across the hardwood flooring.

DRESSED IN dry clothing, she was racing again, this time for the mudroom, where she slipped on a rain jacket, flipping the hood onto her head. She grabbed an extra jacket off the wall peg and ran through the cabin again. Mushy bounded right by her side, believing their running through the house was a new game. Doggy high spirits ended on the front porch as Tracker commanded him to stay, then jumped down the steps and sprinted for the truck. Mushy sat down on his haunches, whimpering throatily, as the truck drove out at gravel-flinging speed.

No way would Benny be at the designated meeting place. Not only did he have a long way to walk, he also had a storm to plow through. Both things meant that she had more than enough time to go to her dad's and find out how the hunt for Uncle Bert had been going before the storm hit. Damn, she was really worried about that old man. Why, God only knew. But Uncle Bert was family. And in the Chippewa view of things, family was everything.

DAVID DROPPED Joey and Mel off at the police station, both making beelines for their trucks. Seconds later both officers were roaring out, headed for home and dry clothing. David and Michael badly needed the very same thing.

"Hey," Michael said, as soon as they were inside David's house, "this is a pretty decent place."

David didn't miss the note of surprise in the deputy's tone. Tossing the truck keys on the hallway table, he grunted, "My bedroom's upstairs." Michael was still looking the place over as he followed David.

"DON'T YOU BELIEVE in coat hangers?"

David pulled out a clean but heavily wrinkled flannel shirt from a plastic basket, tossing it to Michael, who caught it. "I don't need coat hangers."

"But," Michael persisted, "you've got a closet. And there's a pole in there begging for coat hangers. You really ought to think about it."

David shrugged off his shirt, then peeled the soaked undershirt over his head. Angrily balling up the sopping T-shirt, he flung it against the wall. "Look, man," David yelled, "don't come into my place telling me how to live, okay?" Michael's gaze was locked on David's bare, very impressive chest. He didn't have much experience with Indians, but a little voice inside his head warned him that getting into an argument about good housekeeping with this particular Indian wasn't entirely wise.

"I was only offering a suggestion."

David was still riled. "You can shove any and all future suggestions. Got it?"

"Yeah."

"Good. Now hurry up. We've got to get going."

MICHAEL HAD more suggestions, mainly about just where they should be going and what they should be doing. None of those involved an old rust-eaten

Toyota that when running, sounded as if its engine was on its last gasp. The car was now mercifully silent, parked alongside a road with a series of homes and trailer houses in what passed for a neighborhood. The gale-force winds whistled around the car as rain pelted the roof, sounding like pebbles hitting a tin can. The noise was beginning to give Michael a headache, yet the police chief didn't appear bothered as he sat in the driver's seat chain-smoking, his eyes glued to one of the houses. After five minutes Michael, a nonsmoker, desperately needed fresh air. He was denied this as the window hadn't a crank handle, merely a gaping hole in the door panel where a handle had once been.

He was worrying about having inhaled a year's worth of secondhand smoke when someone wearing a rain slicker came out of one of the houses. The figure hurried toward a truck, hopped in, and took off. Cigarette stuck in the corner of his mouth, eyes squinting against the smoke, the Indian cop keyed the ignition while vigorously pumping the accelerator. Eventually the Toyota wheezed into life.

"Is it all right to ask where we're going?"

"No."

Michael shook his head, then watched as a duck waddled along the edge of the road. The duck was passing them. He glanced back at David. "Think we could go wherever it is we're going just a smidgen faster?"

"This is as fast as it gets, chum." David flicked ash from his cigarette without bothering to aim for the overflowing pop-out ashtray. Then in a completely deadpan voice he cracked wise. "But hey, if it helps ease your burning impatience, what don'tcha just try pretending you're in an Indian funeral procession with only one set of jumper cables."

Michael knew there was supposed to be a joke somewhere in there. "I don't get it," he finally said.

David laughed. "No, don't expect you do." He glanced at Michael, then back again to the road ahead. "You kinda have to be a ragged-ass blanket Indian to get that one."

THE WINDSHIELD WIPERS didn't work any better than the missing window crank, but the sheets of rain kept the windshield reasonably clear. The thing that made Michael edgy was David's driving without the aid of the car's headlights. Oh, he understood they were tailing someone, but the low-hanging storm clouds and the tall trees lining both sides of the two-lane road had effectively reduced daylight to pitch. Illumination—a weakened flashlight beam, a fired tracer round—would be most welcome in the nearly total darkness. But David kept the Toyota putting along. Finally he slowed the car to a stop and put an end to the engine's misery.

The storm was moving rapidly off to the south, gray daylight leaking through the scudding cloud cover. On both sides of the road enormous trees swayed. The rain beating on the tin-can roof slackened to a steady thrum and the car was only now and again buffeted by a gust of wind. Michael still couldn't see beyond the curve of the car's hood, yet he sensed David could. And David's unblinking stare never wavered from whatever he was watching.

Being left out of the loop was a thing Michael simply could not tolerate. He'd tried nearly all of his moves on David—charm, heavy-handedness, even the "I'm following you, pal" move. All had earned him squat. Digging around for yet another tactic, he came up with cordiality. Michael wasn't good at cordial, but he decided to give it a fling. Clearing his throat, he said, "You guys have many problems with bears up here on the rez?"

"Sure do," David answered tonelessly.

Well, the two-word answer was better than nothing. Michael tried to keep the banal conversation alive. "You kill many?"

"Not me." David stirred, shifting his weight, his arm remaining on the steering wheel. He did not avert his gaze from what he was watching. "I'm not allowed to kill bears."

"Why not?"

"I'm Bear Clan."

"Oh, yeah. You bet." Michael hoped that made

him sound as if he thoroughly understood. He didn't.

David wasn't fooled. His eyes flicked toward the deputy, then back toward the windshield. "Bear Clan people aren't allowed to kill bears."

"Oh, yeah, gotcha. But hey? What happens if a bear decides it wants to kill you?"

"In that case, whatever happens is fair."

Interested now, Michael asked, "Have you ever had to...you know, go with self-defense?"

David held up a hand with two fingers upraised. "Twice."

Michael's eyes bulged slightly. "Hey! No shit? How'd that work out?"

David cupped his hands around the Bic, lighting yet another cigarette. Blowing smoke, he said, "Pretty good."

Michael was rapidly beginning to realize just how much he loathed Indian humor.

The silence returned and time dragged on. This, Michael determined, was the worst surveillance duty he'd ever pulled. Not only was he not told who they were tailing, they'd done most of the tailing in a car that couldn't outrun a duck. Now here he was stuck in the woods with bears lurking behind every tree. What really began to gnaw was the mounting certainty that his chain-smoking Bear Clan Indian companion wouldn't necessarily feel compelled to jump in should a bear decide to maul anyone other than himself.

Oh, yeah. This is great duty. Mama, give me more.

Michael sat up straight the instant he saw the small distant glow; it lasted only one or two seconds, then was gone. As if this was the cue he'd been waiting for, David zipped up his jacket and opened the car door. The Toyota, along with its many other minuses, didn't have interior lighting. As David stepped out, he made a throwaway comment about bears looking for lunch. Then he was gone.

BENNY WAS DRYING HIS hair with a hand towel and Tracker was so intent in what she had to tell him that when the passenger door suddenly opened, both of them started. Her eyes were as wide as saucers as David slid in, causing Benny to move further along the bench, squeeze in against Tracker.

After quickly closing the door, David said, "So how's it goin', eh?"

For several seconds, Tracker didn't remember to breathe. When at last the need overwhelmed her, she swallowed a great gulp. "Where did you come from?" she cried.

David used his thumb to point behind him, through the rear window. "Little ways down the road."

"You followed me?" She sounded mortified.

"Yep."

"Alone?"

"Nope. Super deputy's with me. But not to worry. He'll stay put. I think our boy's kinda afraid of the woods."

Benny stared down at the damp towel in his hands, his expression utterly defeated. In a small voice he asked, "You gonna put the cuffs on me, David?"

David and Tracker made eye contact over Benny's bowed head. Without breaking that contact, he said, "I was thinking maybe we'd have a beer first."

Benny immediately perked. "I'm starvin', ya know. Think maybe we could have that beer over in Cornucopia?"

David considered the request, thinking about the bar called Fish Lipps. Shaking his head he said, "Don't think that's such a good idea. Too many folks we know hang out in the Lipps."

"What about C-Side?" Tracker suggested.

David put the kibosh on that one, too. "Naw, Chuck and Sig took off again for Delta. That means C-Side's gonna stay buttoned up for a couple of weeks."

Benny was no longer meek natured. "But, man, I'm hungry. And I mean belly-snappin'-at-my-liver hungry." He lip-pointed to Tracker. "This here girl not only ate most of my lunch, she had me hauling my sorry butt over some real bad ground in the middle of a mother of a storm. If you don't feed me, David, I'm gonna file a cruel and unusual on ya."

David laughed. "Tell ya what, I'll spring for a big plate of nachos over at Jack's."

Benny shook his head woefully, heaved a huge sigh. "I was hoping for a plate of bloody meat." He sighed again. "But if all you've got is Jack's nachos...well, I guess I am your prisoner."

"Hey!" David laughed again. "Ya think?"

Tracker started the truck as David hopped out. Just before closing the door he yelled, "Don't drive too fast. I'll be following in the rollin' wreck."

Nodding that she understood, Tracker slid the gears into first, setting off at a snail's pace for Washburn.

MICHAEL WAS NEVER so relieved to see anyone in his entire life. During the eternity he'd had to wait, he'd heard all kinds of noises beyond the Toyota's thin aluminum walls. Noises that had nothing to do with the lessening wind and rain. They were sounds made by mammals—big suckers, and every last one of them equipped with pointy claws and long sharp teeth. Michael now knew exactly what it felt like to be a slab of Spam in an easy-open can.

"Where the hell have you been?" he cried.

Sliding in and closing the door, David keyed the ignition. "Steady, boy. I'm here now, you're saved."

He took a quick look at the deputy. "You sound like you could use a drink."

"Damn right I could," Michael snorted.

"Will a beer do ya?"

"A six-pack would be better."

David turned on the headlights as the car began its sluggish roll. "Then you just hang in there, chum. Tonto knows just the place."

MICHAEL DIDN'T RECOGNIZE Tracker's parked truck as they passed it, David maneuvering the Toyota up the sloping dirt-and-gravel parking lot behind the Cantina del Norte bar. Michael had never been inside the Washburn watering hole simply referred to by the locals as Jack's. Until this very minute, Michael hadn't felt any deep inner longing to rub elbows with the locals. All he'd wanted was to serve his time in law enforcement hell, then run like a scalded dog back to Madison. But today had been a pip. He hadn't been kidding about needing a six-pack. Seconds after David parked the car under a leafless tree—its branches clawing the top of the car like fingernails screeching down a chalkboard—Michael leaped out and slammed the door, going for all he was worth up the hill that ended at the bar's back door.

TEN

TRACKER CHOSE the table near the kitchen doorway. The bar was an honest-to-God ship's bow, complete with a carved wooden masthead—a woman in eighteenth-century dress, skirts billowing behind her, standing on the crest of a wave. Jack, the owner of the Cantina del Norte, had placed a black sombrero on the woman's head. Somehow the thing made her look, well, jaunty. As was usual for this time of day, the bar was packed. Jack, in his mid-forties and rakishly good looking, was behind the bar under the mizzenmast, standing in his typical pose: one leg raised, foot resting on the cooler. He was wearing a green Packers T-shirt, tan Bermuda shorts, and gray yachting sneakers. The weather just outside the barroom windows was cold and blowing, but the calendar on the wall above the cash register read spring. Jack preferred to believe in the things he read rather than in the things he actually experienced.

His smile seemed genuine, but his eyes were empty as he continually flicked the ash off a cigarette. From the other side of the bar, the pub babble flowed. A longtime bartender, Jack knew just when to give a consoling nod during an all-too-familiar sob story, just when to laugh at a well-worn joke. At the moment the object of conversation in the bar was a retriever, the dog's owner taking a poll on whether the dog should be put down. Differing opinions were flying as Tracker and Benny slipped in through the back door, made their way along the curve of the bar and into the darker area of the barroom. The only soul to notice their entrance was Jack, his blue eyes coming alive with mild surprise as he lifted his chin—Jack's way of saying hello.

At the table bolted against the wall, Benny, still wearing his hood up, hiked himself into a chair. In the murky light provided by the long Miller Lite bottle lamp hanging over the only pool table, Benny looked like a ghoul. Just as Tracker sat in the other chair, Lois, a longtime employee of Jack's, poked her blond head out of the kitchen doorway, about to yell at Jack. Before Lois could let fly, Tracker hurriedly ordered a large platter of del Norte's infamous black bean nachos and two regular Millers. Lois signaled the okay on the nachos, but she testily yelled the beer order over to Jack. Without so much as a turn of his curly head, and still managing to seem immersed in the discussion about the dog, he drew out the cans of brew, popped the tops, and walked to the end of the bar. Setting the cans on the counter, he hollered, "Here ya go, Track."

She left Benny at the table, going to fetch the beers just as Jack sauntered back to his place. Tracker wasn't what anyone would call a del Norte regular, and whenever she deigned to put in an appearance Jack ordinarily would give her his full attention. But at the moment he was concerned about the retriever's owner. The man was getting loud, drowning out the three TVs and the jukebox (on which someone had punched the gravelly voiced Rod Stewart). Not even combined could the Weather Channel (first TV), a CNN talking head's account of some disaster or other (second TV), an announcer baying, "Emily Hewitt, come on down!" (third TV), and Rod screaming and shouting his juked sexual excitement for Hot Legs equal the din created by one thoroughly inebriated Wisconsin duck hunter.

"Fuckin' dog! Cost me three hundred bucks an' all the damn thing does is dig up gophers and chipmunks, leaving me to beat off the mean and the quick ones. What I oughta do is shoot the sucker, then go after the little bastard that stuck me with him. Kinda teach both of 'em a lesson, ya know?"

Jack kept a baseball bat under the counter but preferred diplomacy over the St. Louie swing. "Hey, I'm widchew, chum." The man sipped his beer, anger momentarily cooling, and Jack, foot once again propped on the cooler, watched him.

THE HOOD PUSHED BACK against his shoulders, Benny assaulted the platter of nachos, shoveling loaded tortilla chips into his mouth at high speed. Tracker took a long pull on her beer. A million questions banged around inside her head, but she knew Benny wouldn't be ready to talk until he'd eaten himself full. Then, too, it was best to wait for David. Being in the del Norte and waiting for David struck her with such a sense of déjà vu that her stomach began to pitch like a herring boat caught out in a Superior squall. This little table in the Cantina was exactly where it had all happened: their fight, the big bust-up.

Non-Indians labor under the misconception that a male Indian's war cry is a bloodcurdling whoop. Indians know better. Know that any male Indian finding himself stuck in deep do-do bellows the fabled four words: *Baby, let me 'splain!* David had done a lot of explaining that night, most of it down on his knees begging her to believe him. Tracker hadn't then, still didn't now.

As she was thinking of the devil, he walked in through the back door; trailing after him was the Bayfield County deputy. David paused behind the bar, speaking to Jack. Evidently he was asking about her because Jack, with a toss of his head, indicated where she could be found. David mouthed his thanks. As he came toward her, time blurred. Tracker was struggling to breathe when he came to stand in front of her, both hands shoved deep inside jeans pockets. Then he was asking a question she'd heard many times before.

"You okay on smokes, babe?"

Tracker could only stare up at him, shake her head. David turned, going to the cigarette machine. She watched, eyes misting, as he fed the machine quarters, punched her brand. Meanwhile, Michael, on the other side of the table, slid into the vacant high chair, nodding to the man beside him.

"Hey, how's it going?"

"Everything's all right." Benny shoveled more food into his mouth.

David went to the bar, retrieved two cans of Leinenkugel, came back to the table, edged into the chair next to Tracker, and shoved one of the cans across to Michael, who picked it up and proceeded to chug it down. Tracker's hands shook as she opened the cigarettes, pulled one out, leaned into the flame David offered. She inhaled, then blew smoke toward the ceiling. In the low-key Chippewa way of doing things, she began a conversation with a topic certain to ease the moment.

"Heard you got a new rifle."

David made himself more comfortable, his shoulder pressing against hers. "Oh, yeah? Who told you about my new rifle? Your dad?"

Tracker shrugged. "He mentioned you'd been going to the sand pit. I put it together the reason had to be a new rifle. Your old one hasn't needed to be sighted in since…'' Her voice trailed off as she feigned trying to remember. She snapped her fingers as if it had suddenly come to her. "Oh, yeah. Since I was at school in the Cities and you were running around behind my back with Sharrie Du Bois.''

David pulled a face, drank some of his beer. The moment dragged. Then, elbows braced against the tabletop, his face inches from hers, he began speaking as if he hadn't heard the dig. "I got a .270 New England with a Swift 1.5 X 4.5 variable scope. I'm using 130-grain rounds.''

Tracker nodded. "Sounds good.''

"Yeah,'' he agreed. "It'd be better if I could sight in the son of a bitch. Even at a hundred yards and with the crosshairs bang on, the sucker shoots high right.''

"Too high for a shoulder?''

As this was Tracker of innumerable neck shots asking, David fiddled with the baseball cap on his head, sounded a derisive laugh. "Duh!''

Michael, not a subsistence hunter, was bored. The first thing he'd learned after being assigned to the backwoods was that when one was bellying up beside a roadhouse sweetie, the jeans-and-flannel-wearing femme fatale invariably asked, "What do you shoot?'' Michael left the table, going for the bar and another round of beers.

Benny pushed the cleaned platter away, leaned

forward. Lip pointing in the direction of Michael's back, he said, "He don't know who I am?"

David didn't bother to hide the smirk. "Not a clue."

Benny eased against the chair's backrest, propping an elbow on the edge of the table. Thoughtful, index finger slowly rubbing across chin, Benny drawled, "Well, damn, this is different."

David, exhaling a long plume of smoke, laughed, "Kinda thought you'd like it."

The effect of the beer and the familiar circumstance were beginning to make Tracker feel a bit too warm all over. Before she found herself yielding to the temptation of slipping her arm through David's, she leaned forward, spoke to Benny. "Let's take him through the mystery of the log barge."

"Are you back on that?" David yelped.

Tracker slapped David's arm and snarled, "Will you please just give me five damn minutes?"

David flashed his killer smile. "Okay, babe. I'd be more than happy to give ya four hours, but if all you're needing is five minutes, I swear to ya, honey, I'll be as quick as I can."

Irked, Tracker slapped his arm again. Watching them, Benny smiled.

"PUTTIN' FRENCHETTE ON the logging recovery deal was like lettin' the fox guard the chickens," the stranger at the table was saying.

Michael carefully placed the beers on the checkerboard-sized table. He had to be careful. His hands were small for a man's (his worst physical flaw in his view), and the table was already littered with two full ashtrays, a platter, and four empty beer cans. As soon as he put the beers down, the stranger hooked one and kept right on talking. Michael eased into the chair as the pair across from him grabbed beers for themselves without bothering to acknowledge his efforts.

"Here comes the best part," Tracker said to David.

The noise level in the bar rose another decibel. The volume of Benny's voice did not rise with it. He simply leaned forward more, the remaining three leaning in with him, four heads meeting at the center of the tiny table.

"All the bullshit Frenchette laid out during his campaign on putting a stop to the salvaging was just that. I told anybody who'd listen that the man was crooked as a hound's hind leg. But hell, he won tribal chair anyway, so I says to myself, okay, that's that. How much harm can the man do in a two-year term? But if what Tracker seen out in the Raspberry's got anything to do with Frenchette, then that man's found a way to hurt us all pretty damn bad."

"You think that recovery operation's gonna hurt the tribe?"

"Dumb question, David," Benny sneered. "Means

you know beans about how this land of ours got stripped down to nothing much more than little piss-ant birches and tags. Them ain't trees, they're friggin' weeds. What we got now ain't nothing like the forests our grandfathers used to walk and hunt in.''

Benny was becoming loud, attracting undue attention. Tracker reached across and touched his hand, flicking her eyes in the direction of the men seated at the bar, who were blatantly eavesdropping. It hadn't been too long ago that men exactly like the ones now in the Cantina were contesting Indian claims on the grounds that Indians already had too many rights. Benny took the hint and lowered his voice.

''The thing you're missin','' he continued, addressing David, ''is that right now ain't the time to recover so much as a sunken toothpick. The weather's all wrong and the lake's a bad, bad lady in the spring. So those boys gotta be recovering something that ain't sunk. I got a good guess on what that is, and it ain't in the bottom of nothing.''

''What the hell are you talking about?'' David cried.

Benny squirmed in the chair, came in closer, his voice low. ''I'm talking about the old growth stand just shy of Raspberry that's—''

David's temper blew. ''Oh, come on! I know that stand. Hell, everybody knows that stand. It's sacred,

Ben. Nobody, and I mean nobody, would ever dare touch it.''

"Oh, yeah?" Benny's tone was a dare. "How do you know? Have you been out there lately? Do you know anybody that has?"

"No," David said tersely. "Have you?"

"Nope. But that's where me an' Track were headed when you popped in on us. An' that's where we'll go right now if you can put off arresting me for a couple more hours."

Michael's ears suddenly perked. "Arrest you! Arrest you for what?"

Benny offered his hand to Michael, his expression and voice deadpan. "I'm Benny Peliquin. Thanks for the beer, eh."

TRACKER WAS fighting back laughter as they all piled into her truck. The deputy was so near hysterical she wouldn't have been at all surprised if David suddenly wrestled him to the ground and wedged a tongue depressor inside his mouth. There was only one jump seat and floor space in the back. Michael and David ignored the jump seat, both choosing instead to sit on the floor with their legs tucked against their chests.

"We have our own way of doing things," David said.

"Yes," Michael countered, "but there is this tricky little item known as following procedure. You show me anywhere in the regs where it states a murder suspect has the right to scarf nachos and beer and I'll eat the damn page!''

Silence reigned while David tried to make himself more comfortable in the confined space. Then Tracker and Benny heard David say in a musing tone, "You're kinda an anal guy, aren't ya?''

EVERYONE ON RED CLIFF knew Tracker's truck on sight. As they drove along Blueberry Road, drivers sailing by in the opposite lane flashed the Red Cliff wave. She waved back, ignoring any and all stares directed at her hooded passenger. No one could see David's or Michael's heads just below the porthole-sized rear windows. The afternoon sky was clearing, sun now dominating the sky, and with each curve of the road came another heart-stopping view. Like migrating birds, artists of every ability annually flocked into Bayfield County. And not one of them has ever managed to capture on canvas or paper the unabashed beauty of Northern Wisconsin.

Reaching Red Cliff's firing range, the sand pit, Tracker negotiated the path ending at the pit's edge. From this point on, they'd be walking. Getting out of the sand pit, which was huge, meant scrambling up the sandy wall, then heading due north through a dense thicket of skinny poplars, birches, and tag alders. Waist-high raspberry bushes, denuded clusters of spiky sticks, were a hazard, every limb eager to rake exposed skin. Benny walked to the far left. Tracker could see him now and again through the tree line. When she heard him cry *"Ho-wah!"* she immediately veered in his direction.

David and Michael followed Tracker. Within minutes they found Benny standing in the middle of a road, one that shouldn't have been anywhere near Raspberry Point. Admittedly it wasn't much of a road. Not even a four-wheeler could have driven over the smashed-down saplings and bramble and widely grooved imprints created by the huge tires of a skidder—a log-pushing piece of equipment. There was a legally running pulp operation less than a couple of miles away, where a skidder was known to be working. Finding evidence of a skidder where it clearly shouldn't have been caused David's heart to thump in his chest.

"What the hell's going on?" Michael demanded.

David turned a bloodless face toward him. "Not now, man...not now."

The four began walking again, Benny well out in front. No one spoke as they hiked along the treacherous path. Little more than half an hour later, they cleared the top of the knoll. What they should have seen from this vantage point were hundreds of enormous white pines, darkened boughs crowding against the clear late-afternoon sky. What they should not have been seeing, but most certainly did, was sunlight glimmering off Lake Superior. Like sleepwalkers, the four continued forward until they reached the edge of unbelievable desolation.

David was the first to come to a semblance of reason, to understand that what they saw was real, not a buck-wild nightmare. His reaction came in a shout. "Holy shit!"

Tracker wanted to do a bit of yelling herself. Trouble was, her throat was locked and her brain refused to register the sight her eyes were taking in. Her feet began to move, taking her slowly along the border of what had been sacred ground. Like an automaton she stepped over and through heavy layers of ankle-breaking slash. When a berm became impassable, still numb from the neck down, she shifted her course, walking along a muddy rut. The skidder was long gone, as were the chain saws. There was no noise now, not even in the winds whipping at her clothing, swirling strands of hair around her face. Finally the heartbreak was too much and she crumbled.

SHE HAD NO concept of time, had no idea how long she pressed her face against the earth, watered the clay with her tears. Hands captured her quaking shoulders and she dimly realized that she was being lifted to her feet. Still weak, she swayed. Strong arms caught her, encircled her. Like a frantic animal she grabbed for the strength the other offered and held on tight.

"We'll get 'em, babe," David said, resting his chin on her head. "I swear to God, we'll get 'em."

MICHAEL'S NORMALLY glib tongue was silenced as he strode several yards behind them. Tracker was glad. This meant that he too was affected by the destruction. Head down, she walked close behind Benny, fighting off the urge to look left or right. New forests are full of sapling and fern ground clutter, but old growth forests are carpeted by nothing more than pine straw. This is because the huge boughs keep the floor in perpetual shade. Tracker remembered this old forest as it had been just last summer, with its mighty branches forming a canopy that rivaled the vaulted ceilings of the world's most impressive cathedrals, and its blessing of cooling shade on the hottest days.

In this new emptiness, the sun's brightness stung her eyes, filled her with an indescribable grief. She willed herself to focus, concentrate hard, for even in this chaos, there was a seam of order, a logical progression. Decimating a forest, particularly if the decimating was done in absolute secrecy, required planning. And money.

Lots of money.

ELEVEN

THEY STOOD dangerously close to the cliff's edge, their bodies buffeted by winds that first skimmed the icy surface of Lake Superior, then surged straight up the jagged cliff wall. Tracker's hearing had returned, the winds now whistling shrilly against her ears.

Covering her ears with her hands, blocking both the wind and the numbing cold, she shouted, "The barge wasn't recovering."

David hunched his shoulders against the wind. "Well, hell, Track, even I figured that one out."

Benny, one hand clamping the hood to his head, lifted his chin, indicating an area a little less than thirty yards away. "Right there is where the logs were skidded over the side. Looks like they did all the cuttin' in the winter when there was a guarantee no one would be coming up here. All they had to do after that was wait for the thaw an' bring the barge in to pull up a prime load of number one Clear. Easy beans."

"Hang on a second," Michael shouted over a

gust of wind. "I'm having some trouble with a few details. Just what is number one clear?"

Experiencing a new pang of grief, Tracker remained silent, turned to face the Big Lake. David took a deep breath, expelled it, then answered the question.

"Number one clear is timber that runs with a perfect grain. In other words, it's lumberyard dream wood. In the late 1800s old growth was cut down like grass, leaving only a few pockets of ancient trees. This particular stand belonged to the Tribe and was visited only twice a year, while the other stands are in the National Forest and are regularly patrolled. So if anyone was looking for trees wide as a man is tall and stretching up five hundred feet, this little isolated section would spring to mind. Especially when foreign markets are willing to pay millions for that grade of timber."

Michael said pensively, "Based on that, it's even harder for me to believe a bunch of tree rustlers would come in here and wipe the place out before they had a guaranteed buyer. The risk factor wouldn't be worth the effort because we're talking about a whole lot of Indians who would be hugely pissed the minute they realized they'd been ripped off. And then there's the fact that any buyer is going to insist on a guarantee of delivery. Guarantees mean contracts. Now how the hell would anybody get anything legally binding on a load of hot lumber?''

Michael's question hung in the chilly air until Benny finally mused aloud, "Ya know, before somebody did the world a favor, I once had a cousin who was the Tribal Attorney.''

FOR A HARD-CORE COP, Deputy Bjorke seemed to be getting the hang of arrest Indian style. During the drive back to Tracker's cabin, David rode shotgun, the deputy and Benny crouched out of sight in the minicab. Pulling into her drive Tracker fully expected Mushy to come bounding off the porch, barking a greeting. Opening the truck's door, she heard Mushy barking, but he wasn't on the porch. Stepping out, staying close to the front of the truck, she saw her dog, heard his barking, but the sound was muffled because Mushy was barking from behind the glass of the cabin's large front window.

David, standing on the opposite side of the truck, looked across the hood to her. "Who do you know who could trap Mush inside your house without getting killed in the effort?''

At a loss for an answer, Tracker locked eyes with him.

Getting anxious, David prodded, "Your dad, maybe?''

Tracker shook her head, said in a low voice, "He swears Mush's an incurable biter. Dad sometimes won't even get out of his truck until I've chained Mushy.'' She looked around. There were no recently made car or truck tire markings in the drive.

David was studying the cabin, the dog trapped inside sounding louder. This was not good. He removed his pistol from the holster, checked the cylinder, snapped it closed. "Stay here."

"But it's my cabin."

David began to move away. "Don't fool with me, woman. I mean it. Stay here."

GUN IN BOTH HANDS held stiff-armed and off to the side, David approached the cabin. Tracker, worrying a thumbnail as she watched him, heard the cab's door open and then someone whispering.

"Track?" Michael had only in the last hour began calling her by the familiar nickname. "Stay exactly where you are and you'll block any sight of me from the windows. I'm gonna slip left to give David some backup."

Tracker's nod was barely perceptible as the door behind her clicked closed. A heartbeat later she heard a faint rustling. Peripherally, she saw Michael slip across the yard; then she lost sight of him until he came to stand amid the scrawny maples lining the drive. The Glock Michael carried was held firmly in both hands, arms extended and locked at the elbows as he sighted down her very own front door. Meanwhile David neared the porch steps. He looked so handsome.

So vulnerable.

DOCTOR OR NOT, Ricky was a tobacco addict. He made no excuses or offered apologies for the vice. In Cherokee his attitude is known as *Sgidvnusdi,* "That's just the way it is." He had no idea how the expression for national Indian fatalism was said in Ojibway, nor did he particularly care. It was far too late to care. Far too late to learn to speak Chippewa beyond the usual hello and good-bye. Doc Ricky was smoking furiously as he packed. Then the bedside phone began to ring. He quickly checked Caller ID, then answered, speaking tersely. "What are you doing?"

Wanda, his assistant, was sobbing, quickly approaching hysterics.

Doc Ricky ran a hand through his hair, breathed heavily into the receiver. "Look, we've been all through this—"

"You don't understand!" she shrieked. "You've got to listen!"

Ricky had neither the time nor the tolerance to endure another of Wanda's weeping jags. "I've gotta go, Wanda."

"Please!" he heard her wail as he slammed the phone down.

IN HIS HOME OFFICE, the door firmly closed against his sharp-eared wife, Tribal Chairman Perry Frenchette made a phone call. After two rings, his cousin-in-law Thelma answered.

"Just wanted to check on you. Find out how you're doing."

Thelma sighed dramatically. "Oh, this has just been the most terrible day. I've tried to nap, ya know? But every time I close my eyes—"

"Yes, I'm sure," Perry snapped, not at all interested in Thelma's inability to nap. Hunching forward, one hand cupped around the mouthpiece, he began speaking in a low, urgent tone. "Thelma, there's something I need you to do."

"Me?" she squeaked.

"Yes, you. You're the only person I trust completely."

Thelma didn't know whether to be flattered or terribly afraid.

ELLIOTT RAVEN FELT that if he had to explain to the county sheriff one more time that he didn't know where David or the sheriff's deputy had gone, he would explode. He'd sent out Mel and Joey to find them and that was the best he could do. Now he had to get on with locating the runaway widow. Not equipped with a detective's cagey mind, Elliott did what came naturally. He called information in

Oklahoma. Hey, why not? Information was free, and as the P.D. was forced to survive on a tight budget, free was real good.

SHERIFF BOTHWELL poured himself yet another cup of coffee, the last stuff in the old pot. He grimaced as he drank the overcooked muck, blatantly eaves-dropping on the dispatcher's one-sided telephone conversations.

FREDDY HAROLD HAD caught hell because of that little girl being a witness. Now what she had or hadn't seen no longer seemed to matter because the wood was out of the water and safely hidden in the lumberyard in Ashland. So in essence, Freddy's most lucrative job to date was finished. The big boss had been something of a comfort to Freddy when he said that because Freddy had run the old man deep into the woods and the old man hadn't been seen or heard from in days, he'd most probably died of exposure. Which was a good thing, because once the body was found, the whole thing would look just like some old Indian fart's way of dying. Old people, the boss said, wandered off and died all the time. He'd said it was because of old-timer's disease.

On the matter of the girl, the boss had not been understanding at all. He'd yelled at Freddy, said he was nothing more than a brainless ape. The boss had gone on to say that the girl was now working with the police. The boss had given Freddy the girl's name, Tracker. What a dumb name for a girl. But knowing her name hadn't helped Freddy find her. While the last of the logs were being lifted, he'd driven around the small rez reading the names printed on the mailboxes. Not one of them had Tracker on it. He was tempted to simply come right out and ask questions about her, but even with his limited deductive skills, he had figured out that on an Indian reservation the Indians would take it entirely amiss that a big white man was inquiring about where to find one of their own. Now that the logs were safe, the big boss no longer seemed concerned about the girl. But because the operation's security was Freddy's job and the girl had breached that security, her living to talk about it severely damaged Freddy's reputation.

That's the thing that made Freddy just as mad as mad could be. His reputation as a bad guy was all he had, the only thing that earned him good money when other guys a whole lot smarter than he was worked as minimum-wage help in restaurant kitchens. If he couldn't find that girl and shut her up for good, he might as well get used to a life of dishpan hands. This possibility was why he was currently spending big in the Isle Vista Casino, in the bar area known as the Lanes. Freddy was being very friendly with the Indians seated at Mug Row, listening to the stories the Indian commercial fishermen told. It was

clear their stories were meant to be jokes because
the Indians all laughed like crazy. Freddy didn't understand half of what was being said, but he laughed
heartily anyway. Then bought another round of
beers, nodding as if he understood when the Indians
all said, *Megwiitch!*

THE TRIBAL COURTHOUSE was completely shut
down when C. Clarence Begay unlocked the front
door with a purloined key and slipped inside. For a
good half hour he'd been a busy boy.

He wasn't busy anymore.

Expression thoroughly surprised, C. Clarence now
lay flat on his back, staring sightlessly at the ceiling,
his green chile-loving form less than a foot away
from the taped outline of the recently deceased tribal
attorney. Within the taped outline, a black stain had
settled deep into the new powder blue carpeting.
Now a fresher stain marked the woof and weave.
The new carpet stain was caused by the small black
hole in between C. Clarence's bushy eyebrows. The
neat round hole was deceptive. The back section of
C. Clarence's skull had been blown apart. Now not
only would the office need new carpeting, because
of the recent grisly wall spatter, it would also need
a few licks of paint.

IMOGEN WAS physically and emotionally exhausted.
Her mother had taken over her lively children, leav-

ing Imogen perched like a bird on the living room couch and holding a cup of hot tea in her shaking hands. She'd been inside the safety of her parents' home less than five minutes when the phone started ringing. She did not need to be told that the call was from Wisconsin. She'd known that simply by the coldness in her father's tone. Now, sipping the tea without tasting it, she tried to take in what he was saying, tried with no success to fit together the jumble of words, make some sense of them. Then her father hung up. He turned to stare at her for a moment, then lifted the receiver and placed a call. Unfortunately, this second conversation she understood only too well.

"Yes, Northwest? I'd like to make two reservations for tomorrow morning's flight to Duluth."

DAVID WAS ON the porch's first step and Michael eased out of the scruffy trees, quickly sidestepping in the direction of the far corner of the cabin. Then all hell broke loose as the front door suddenly swung open and Mushy came bounding out. The big dog hit David squarely in the chest, knocking him flat on his back on the ground.

Michael fired.

Tracker screamed.

Then she was running toward David, and Michael averted his aim, raising the gun high just as it fired a second time.

David was cussing at the dog standing squarely on his chest. The dog weighed a ton and David feared his ribs would crack when Tracker appeared, grabbing the dog's thick collar, yelling for him to heel. Through every second of the excitement a wizened, filthy old man watched from the front door, dark eyes wide as saucers.

"WELL, DAMN," Uncle Bert said to the odd foursome. "I was just havin' a nap."

Inside the living room, Benny took over the couch where Old Bert had previously been napping. Michael helped David examine himself for dog bites while Tracker knelt beside Mushy, petting him and repeatedly telling him that he was a good boy.

"Yeah, right," David said snidely.

Tracker rose to Mushy's defense. "Well, he is a good boy! When he saw you coming up to my house with a gun, what was he suppose to think?"

Jerking away from Michael, David shouted, "That dog couldn't think its way out of a soggy paper bag."

"You're only saying that because you know he doesn't like you."

"Well, duh!" David jeered. "How's he suppose to like me after you used my shirt to train him to attack?"

"I used a pair of your jeans," she corrected. "Your shirt wiped up puppy pee."

Michael was confused and in this state of confusion asked, "Hey? Are you guys married?"

Both turned, yelling, *"Gawain!"* (No!)

THE MEN WERE sitting at the trestle table, two on either bench, with Uncle Bert dominating the discussion, while in the kitchen Tracker quickly threw together a pot of coffee. That done, she hurriedly came to sit at the table directly across from her uncle.

"Didn't hear nothin'," Bert said, his tone peeved. "That ain't unusual. My ears are so bad I can't even hear myself snore."

Tracker nodded, knew that her uncle's deafness was the primary cause of his self-imposed isolation. Even though he'd become adept at lip-reading, he hated his disability so much he'd chosen to cut himself off from everything and everyone.

"My boys sure heard something, though," her uncle was saying. Uncle Bert's boys were his pack of horrible hounds. "I thought they was hearing a raccoon or some such, an' I wasn't interested because I was tired because I just got back from fishing. I caught a big string of brownies. I just let my boys go on outside by themselves. They was gone a good long time and I didn't think nothing of that, neither. I was fixing to clean the fish when only two of 'em came back. I went looking for the other boys."

He paused to take a drag off his cigarette, ignoring the overly long ash drooping off the end. Fastidious about such things, Tracker watched the ash as her uncle exhaled and continued with his tale.

"Mostly what I thought was that the boys had tangled with a bear, so I grabbed up my rifle an' followed after the two that'd made it home." The old man shook his head, let go a mournful sigh. The extended ash finally fell from the cigarette, landing on the table, disintegrating just outside the clean ashtray Tracker had slid near enough to catch it.

"My boys are like that," her uncle said, oblivious to the mess, his frowning niece. "Whenever they get into trouble, they come fetch me. I knew them two was taking me to their brothers. They led me straight for the cliffs and I could see 'em running just up aways, but I was lookin' mostly at the ground, checking for bear spoor. I looked up just in time to see Rusty, my best boy, leap straight up like he'd been gut-shot. Then he just flopped over. About that time, Sage, my other boy, got hit. I saw half his poor head get blown clear off."

The saddened old man took a final drag off the cigarette that had burned down to the filter; then he ground it out in the ashtray. Tracker no longer cared that her uncle had made an ashy mess of her polished table. Those dogs of his may have been the bane of everyone else's existence, but they'd been his children. Seeing two of them shot dead would have been like receiving a stab straight through the heart. The old man rubbed a gnarled hand along moistening eyes.

Trying to save him embarrassment, Tracker switched the subject, touching her uncle's hand so that he would look at her, read her lips. "I called Dad." Her uncle nodded, letting her know he understood. Tracker continued. "I told him you were safe. You know, everybody's been out looking for you."

The old man's eyes began to beam mischief as his lips curved in a sly smile. "I expect the ones doing the looking were mostly my enemies." He croaked a wheezy laugh. "Ya know, the day I finally go toes-up, them guys are gonna have no one left to hate. Kinda reckon they'll be the ones who'll miss me most, eh?"

Tracker chuckled with him. Kindness was not the old man's strong suit. Shrugging the moment off, he looked again at David, speaking loudly and vehemently. "I was gonna get them dog killers, Davey. Was gonna shoot 'em deader'n snot. Didn't care if I got hung for it, neither."

Uncle Bert grabbed the pack of cigarettes lying on the table. Taking one out, sticking it in his mouth, he leaned to the side, accepting a light from Benny, his bench mate. Blowing smoke toward the rafters, the old man once again began to rant.

"Anybody low-down enough to shoot a dog ain't

fit to live. That's what I was thinkin' when all of a sudden this big son of a bitch comes out of nowhere. Had to be the biggest Chamook I ever seen in my whole sorry life. Just lookin' at him scared the blue piss right outta me. I was fixin' to draw down on him when three more Chamooks started comin' outta the brush. Four on one ain't fair, so I legged it. I ain't run so fast since I was a kid. I was going for home when I got to thinkin' that I was leading a bunch of strangers straight to where I live. That's when I started running the other way.

"It was after a couple of days of duckin' an' hidin' that I got kinda curious about those fellas, and that's when I slipped back to the cliffs. You kids'll never guess what I saw goin' on down in the bay."

Tracker touched his hand again. When he looked at her she said, "We already know."

The old man gave his niece a scowl. "All right, miss smarty britches, but do you know who I saw right down there with 'em?"

"Could it have been our tribal attorney?"

Bert gleefully slapped the table and howled, "You're not even close, girlie!"

DAVID CALLED the station, checking in. Elliott answered at the first ring. "Except for the sheriff hanging around and driving me screaming damn nuts, everything on this end is real quiet. I'll radio Joey and Mel an' tell 'em I found you, so it's okay for them to go home an' get some rest.''

"No, don't send them home." David spoke hurriedly and Elliott was about to respond with his usual stream of questions when David sidetracked him. "How goes the hunt for our missing widow?"

"That's done," Elliott answered proudly. "Found her with no trouble at all. She's in Oklahoma, but she's comin' back tomorrow. Her dad called me with their flight number an' everything."

"Good job." David paused, collecting his thoughts. "Listen," he finally said, "I've still got a few more things to do and I'm keeping the deputy with me. Before you radio the guys, tell Bothwell to go on back to Washburn. We'll catch up with him in the morning."

Elliott caught on in seconds. Bothwell, seated at the second desk, seemed to be involved with an article in a year-old *Field & Stream* magazine. Elliott wasn't fooled. "Yeah, you do sound pretty bushed," Elliott said. "Why don't you and that deputy go get a hot meal?"

He paused, pretending to be listening as he scribbled on a notepad. Lifting the pad at an angle, looking down and through the bottoms of the bifocals resting on the tip of his bulbous nose, Elliott seemed to be reading back what David had dictated.

"Okay, you're getting a burger at the Lanes, then bunking down at your place. You'll call in around five in the a.m. and you're authorizing overtime for me to keep the shop open.'' Elliott set the pad down, spoke with a smile on his face. "Thanks for the overtime, boss. My wife's gums have been giving her fits and she hates the dentist over at our clinic. Makes me take her all the way to Ashland to see a dentist. Ya know, keepin' that woman's gums in her head is startin' to cost me a whole lot of money. What? Oh...well, talk to ya later then.''

David had been totally captivated by Elliott's improvisational ability. He had just enough time before his dispatcher hung up to say, "Elliott, sometimes you're worth your weight in gold.''

"Ten four, boss.''

As BOTH BENNY and Uncle Bert looked completely done in, Tracker played mother, tucking them in separate beds. She assigned Benny the pull-out couch, Uncle Bert her bedroom. Because he missed his dogs so much, Tracker ordered Mushy to stay, pointing to his pallet she'd just laid out in its usual place at the bottom of her bed. Mushy, with a whipped-dog attitude, got the idea, but just to make certain that he stayed put, Tracker closed the bedroom door.

David was making another call as she came into the main room and caught Michael examining a wide variety of Indian antiques displayed on the wall. He seemed especially taken with the old lacrosse sticks mounted like an X.

She came to stand beside him. "Those belonged to my mother's father," she said. "Back in the twenties, Red Cliff was the only place left in the world where lacrosse was still being played the way it was meant to be played, with very few rules and absolutely no padding or helmets. My grandfather was said to be one of the best players. He once finished a game even though he had to run with a broken leg."

Michael looked obliquely at her. Her expression was impossible to read. But she had to be putting him on. No one could run with a broken leg. He snorted derisively. "That took guts."

"Yes," she replied airily, "guts are a Charboneau trait."

LOATH AS SHE WAS to admit it, sometimes David was just too cool. He'd been extremely cool manipulating the deputy, convincing Michael that it was his very own idea to remain at the cabin in order to safeguard Uncle Bert and their prisoner, Benny.

David had shrugged and said, "Well, if you insist."

Before Michael could think it out, realize that he'd been snookered, David had hustled her out. Now they were on their way to the Tribal Courthouse. They were in her truck, and without asking her permission, David slid behind the steering wheel, turning the key, which was still in the ignition. She was appalled that she'd allowed him to just do that as they sped down the gravel road; white birches lined both sides of the road, ghostly figures illuminated by the truck's high beams.

Tracker finally found her voice. "Won't we be breaking and entering?"

David sent her a brief sideways glance. "Nah. I'm the law, remember?"

In the panel's muted green light she saw his impish grin.

THE TRIBAL police department was normally closed and dark by this time of day, but as the day had been far from normal, lights blazed. Parked on a slant in front of the small building were two tribal patrol cars. Joey's and Mel's. They had either just performed their little errand or Elliott was still trying to explain it to them before they rolled.

In the parking lot just across from the P.D., David killed the lights on Tracker's truck as he steered into the parking lot for the Tribal Courthouse. He stopped at the back of the thoroughly dark building and shut down the engine.

At the front door David held a pin light in his mouth as he inspected the overfull key ring, trying the keys one by one until he finally slipped the correct key into the dead bolt, gave it a turn, and heard the muted *snick*. Pocketing the keys, removing the pin light from his mouth, he turned to whisper a warning. That was when he realized Tracker was no longer standing right behind him. He had no idea how long she'd been gone because when she put her mind to it, she could move with all the noise of a wisp of smoke. "Damn woman," he muttered as he entered the building. Once inside, he made certain the door was locked again. True, he'd effectively locked Tracker out, but if she'd stayed put, that wouldn't have been a problem. He couldn't simply leave the office unlocked due to his fear of someone stumbling in while he was in the act of committing a felony. So wherever she'd gotten to, Tracker was on her own.

WHILE DAVID HAD been fumbling with the keys, Tracker had spotted something irregular just off to the side. Because of the rains, the lawn had been rendered slushy, much too soft to tread upon without doing damage, thus incurring the Tribal Chairman's wrath. But someone had dared to walk on the fragile lawn, someone unconcerned with sinking deep into the mud and trampling down the grass. Someone who preferred to edge along the office's perimeter.

DAVID DIDN'T freely admit this to anyone, but he was largely superstitious. It didn't help his phobia one little bit that the building was as black as the feathering of a death raven or that as he approached the ex-attorney's office he was hit by an odor strong enough to gag a maggot. Cupping his left hand over his mouth and nose, David opened the door with his right.

TWELVE

As TRACKER STOOD outside the building watching David through the partially opened window, one side of her face was bleached by the light of the full moon. David, standing in the glow of a desk lamp, seemed rooted to the carpet as he stared at the floor, his attention fixed on something she couldn't see. To gain his attention, she tapped the windowpane once, then twice. David did not respond. Deciding on a more direct approach, she spoke through the two-inch gap between the sash and frame.

"Hey, sailor. Lookin' for a good time?"

David started violently, slapping a hand against his chest as he yelped, "Son of a bitch!" Catching sight of her, he was furious. "Damn it, Track! How long have you been out there?"

"About a minute." Her tone changed, became crisp. "I don't know what you're doing in there, but I found a lot of stuff out here."

He almost said, "There's a lot of stuff in here, too." Instead he asked, "What sort of stuff?"

"I'm not telling until you give me a hand."

David went to the window, raised it high enough to pull her through. Her feet had barely touched the carpet when the smell hit her like a bomb.

"My God!" she yelped, her hand flying to cover her nose and mouth. Behind this emergency mask she complained, "I can't believe they still haven't cleaned this place."

"They did," he said dryly. "But now they're going to have to clean it all over again."

She gasped sharply, hand falling away from her face. Voice faint, she said, "You mean, there's..."

In the pale light David's eyes seemed impossibly large. "Oh, yeah."

Tracker whispered, "Anyone we know?"

Nodding, David answered, "Uh-huh."

DOC RICKY WAS not handling the current situation at all well. As the P.D. did not have a holding cell, Elliott was worried that the doctor's arm-waving would escalate, push the envelope on an already sticky situation. The tricky part was Mel. He'd stationed himself in front of the door, the office's only means of escape, and eyeing the doctor the entire time, he caressed the butt of his holstered sidearm. If the doctor suddenly decided he didn't want to be under arrest, made an attempt to leave, Elliott knew Mad Mel wouldn't hesitate. He'd shoot Doc Ricky, then giggle over the doctor's corpse. David badly needed to fire Mel. The boy just wasn't right. Elliott's one hope for disaster containment rested on Joey, who was sitting on a desk, speaking to the doctor in calming tones.

"One phone call," Doc Ricky shouted. "I know I have the right to make one phone call."

Languidly, Joey reached behind him, pulling the desk phone within easy reach. The doctor snatched up the receiver, index finger furiously stabbing the phone's buttons.

IT WAS MORE THAN apparent that the Navajo was as dead as a door knocker, that any attempt at resuscitation would be a waste of effort. Given the sight of the recent paper storm, the office files strewn everywhere, it was also obvious that if any incriminating documents regarding the illegal log harvest had been found, they were long gone. David, worried the light had been on too long, that someone over in the P.D. would notice, switched off the lamp, snapped on the pin light, and guided Tracker out. Once they were in the hallway, the Tribal Attorney's door firmly closed behind them, the fresher air helped clear their heads.

"Okay," he said wearily. "What stuff did you find outside?"

"Footprints. Someone went from window to window, probably watching the Navajo."

"The shot that killed him didn't come from any window," David said crisply. "It was too clean."

"I didn't say the shot was fired from the window," she insisted. "I simply said someone went from window to window. That person could have been the killer or just someone trying to get a peek at the murder scene. You know, like a curious kid, maybe."

"I'm not buying that one, Track. Whoever it was wasn't just looking in out of idle curiosity."

Tracker tossed her hands wide, slapped her thighs. A long time ago she learned that whenever David became argumentative, it was best not to feed into his mood.

"All right," David said mostly to himself. "Let's assume that the Navajo was here to get a look at poor old Jud's files. Then let's say Peepers wanted to have a look, too, and surprises said Navajo. Then of course Peepers has to kill him."

"And Peepers did come inside," she said softly.

"How do you know?"

"There's a partial footprint in blood that matches the prints outside."

David removed his cap, scratched the top of his head. "Which would mean Peepers and the killer were after the same thing but weren't exactly on the same team."

"Or, we're back to the curious kid wanting to get a look at a freshly killed person."

Thoroughly frustrated, David slammed the cap back onto his head. "Damn, Track, stay with me on this. Forget the curious kid. There is no curious kid. What we have are two dead guys and about ten tons of missing white pines, and all we have as a near witness to anything is your loony uncle. We need something solid, something written down and—"

Tracker received a brain jolt. "Hildy!"

"What?"

"Hildy," she snapped. "Hildy Blanc!" Tracker took off in a run. Hoping to prevent her from killing herself as she ran the dark hallway, David followed, fixing the narrow beam of his pin light just ahead of her running boots.

HILDY BLANC HAD BEEN the Tribal Court Recorder for decades. Not only did she record all court sessions, she was also responsible for keeping the records for literally everything. Hildy was a good soul but generally thought to be quirky. Actually, what Hildy was, was cunning. She knew that on a small reservation with few job opportunities, the key to her continuous employment lay in her own unique filing system. The harder her system was for anyone else to figure out, the more secure she was in her job when governing councils changed. The tiny office belonging to the Court Recorder had floor-to-ceiling shelves, each shelf stuffed with cryptically encoded files that made absolutely no sense to anyone other than Hildy. Because of the shelves, Hildy's tiny empire had no windows, so Tracker and

MARDI OAKLEY MEDAWAR   203

David could snap on the overhead lighting. After their eyes focused, she and David stood looking at the shelves in horror.

"This will take years," David groaned.

Tracker swallowed her anxiety. "How long can you hold the good doctor before you have to charge him?"

David checked his wristwatch, did a quick mental calculation. "About four more hours."

Tracker took a deep breath, let it go. "Then we just start pulling paper. And neatness doesn't count."

"Thank God."

RECEIVER AGAINST her car, mouth a tight line, Wanda listened. Behind her, her husband sat in the old wingback easy chair. After a long day of pulling a few reservation cars back from the brink of death, then finding ways to hold them together using little more than baling wire, the rez's one and only magical repairman was pure tuckered. He was also sipping a can of beer and getting steadily drunker as he watched television, the volume—as usual—too loud. Even though she knew he couldn't hear due to the television, out of habit, Wanda stole a glance over her shoulder before speaking.

"Why should I help you?" she snarled, her voice low.

"Because I love you."

That was it. The one line able to melt her like butter. Still she remained silent for a moment, letting him squirm.

"Baby?" His voice held a pleading edge.

"Ten minutes," she said. Then she put the phone down.

TRACKER HEARD the front door of the building open, and for a second, she froze. David, on his knees as he rifled through a pile of folders, was oblivious. Tracker really could have used that fraction of a second, but because she'd wasted it, she was unable to close the door to the Court Recorder's cubby before all the lights in reception flashed on. The lights were quickly followed by the sound of footsteps coming along the hallway. Then the footfalls stopped.

"Hello?" a female voice quivering with trepidation hailed. "Is someone here?"

It was David's turn to freeze.

"We're going to have to front this out," Tracker said, her words just a notch above hissing.

Looking up at her, David was thinking quickly, none of the thoughts flitting through his brain good ones. There was another dead body in the Courthouse, and he, as police chief, should be entirely focused on the murder investigation. Instead, he was about to be caught on his knees rifling through tribal records.

David did a bit of hissing of his own. "If you have any idea on just how we can brazen this one out, trust me, I'm all ears."

"You're the law!" she whispered.

His response was notably sarcastic. "Maybe you haven't noticed, but right now I'm a lawman about to be caught in a highly illegal act."

Tracker's eyes hardened. "Sometimes you're just too helpless."

"Is this where you slap me for my own good?"

Making a disgusted sound in the back of her throat, Tracker turned on her heel.

LEGS SHAKING, heart thumping like a drum, Thelma stood in the partially illuminated hall. The Court Recorder's door was open and the lights were on inside. Thelma knew she wasn't imagining the voices. She was not alone in what should be an empty building. Thelma was about to run away when Tracker darted out into the hall. Relief came over her in such a huge wave that Thelma very nearly keeled over. Yet as Tracker came toward her, Thelma rallied. "Do you know you scared me half to death?"

Tracker came to a stop. "Sorry, Thel."

The muttered apology further fueled Thelma's anger. "What are you doing here? And how did you get in when the front doors were locked?"

Before Tracker could answer, both women heard a male voice say, "Thelma, the doors were locked because this is suppose to be a secured crime scene." David showed an indignant face. "You mind telling me what you're doing here this time of night?"

Stepping to the side of Tracker, Thelma was at a loss as she stared at the Tribal Police Chief standing half in, half out of the Recorder's office. Striving to regain the moment, Tracker moved to block Thelma's view of David.

Placing a hand lightly on the woman's trembling arm, she said soothingly, "It's all right. Just answer his question and I'll make certain he doesn't arrest you."

A great respecter of authority, Thelma proceeded to babble. "I'm here because of Perry." Dabbing her eyes with a thoroughly used and wadded piece of tissue that seconds ago had been hidden inside her hand, Thelma sobbed. "I told him I couldn't bring myself to come back inside this place, that I'm about to have a nervous collapse, but he said I'm the only one who can find anything in Hildy's—"

"What?"

David's bark had Thelma jumping almost straight up and straight out of her sensible shoes. Tracker grabbed the older woman's cold hand and rubbed it briskly, sending both warmth and reassurance. Thelma sniffled into the tissue, then meekly squeaked, "Perry told me he needed a file from Hildy's office."

BARELY A MINUTE after managing to put aside her case of the frights, Thelma suffered a relapse. For a space of moments she could only stare in shock at the mess Tracker and David had made of the Court Recorder's little den. Squaring her shoulders enabled Thelma to regain a modicum of her formidable self. She stepped into the breach, a veritable whirlwind of efficiency. Moments later, all of the folders were crammed again in their rightful slots. With the exception of the folder requested by the Tribal Chairman. That folder was clutched against Thelma's well-endowed bosom, as with one eyebrow slightly raised, she began to regard the pair before her with increasing suspicion.

"There's something here that smells just a little funny," she said, eyes shifting between Tracker and David.

"Oh," David said, "that'd be the Navajo."

Tracker kicked his ankle.

But it was far too late to whistle back David's little faux pas. Thelma clutched the folder more tightly as she began cautiously sniffing the air. "My God," she said, a tremulous edge to her voice, "something really does smell bad."

THERE WAS NO DOUBT about it. With the advent of Thelma, the secret of another body in the Tribal Courthouse was well and truly out of the bag. On a brighter note, David now had the file he'd needed.

Having pried it away from Thelma, he whipped through it like a dervish, finding in small print the name of a global company currently being sued in just about every country on the planet for a host of unethical practices.

Nagaki Limited.

That one name had been making national news at least once a week, each piece ending with the same file footage of Japanese businessmen doing their best to dodge cameras while Greenpeacers hollered, ''Planet rapists!'' None of the news reports had ever bothered David before. The Japanese company had only seemed to be bad news for the rain forests and the dolphins. Now his own people were about to feel the brunt of Nagaki's illicit pilfering. Incensed beyond description, David gave the file to Tracker for safekeeping as he loped off to one of the offices to place a rather delayed call.

The line rang and rang.

There was no answer.

THE FIRST SHOT had blasted out the front room's picture window, shards of flying glass inflating the drawn curtains. The shot had missed Michael by inches. Benny, who was sleeping on the couch, instantly woke and rolled off the sleeper bed. More shots came through and Michael and Benny crawled across the bare wood floor, pulling the plugs of all the lamps that were on. Able to see only dimly in the darkened cabin, they scrambled for Tracker's freestanding gun cabinet in the far corner. Michael would never again complain about North Woods women and their passion for guns. In between the sporadic shots, snores could be heard coming from the bedroom.

Blessed are the stone deaf, Michael thought. *For they shall die in their sleep.*

At the cabinet, Michael quickly learned that Tracker wasn't in the habit of keeping the gun cabinet locked for safety. Ordinarily, he would have given her a stern lecture on the subject, but just at the moment he was simply too thankful for her negligence. Benny made a grab for the Winchester 70 just after Michael lifted out the lever-action Winchester 94.

"Ammo's in the drawer," Benny said.

The drawer was heavy, sliding out jerkily after several frantic tugs. A shot slammed into the brace holding up a moose rack and the trophy came down, hitting the floor with an ear-rupturing clatter.

"Oh, man," Benny whined nasally, looking nervously over his shoulder at the ruined treasure, "Track's gonna be so pissed. She took that moose in Canada."

Another round zinged just above their heads and the two men slapped the floor. Then the telephone began to ring. Michael lifted his head just enough to make out Benny's shadowy form. Michael had never, if one discounted the drunk with laughable aim, been in a shoot-out. He was scared half out of his mind, but at the same time flooded with an intense adrenaline rush. Somehow, as the telephone continued to shrill, he managed to keep his voice even. "You wanna get that?"

The antique lamp on a small table exploded, both men protectively covering their heads with their arms. Blissfully unconcerned, the telephone pealed on.

"I don't think it's for me!" Benny yelped.

Rolling onto his back, shoving a shell into the rifle, Michael said, "It's probably a telemarketer anyway."

Benny's rifle was loaded, ready to go. The phone persisted, demanding immediate attention. Benny looked at the telephone with pure disgust. "I hate those guys. Have you ever noticed they always call during the most inconvenient times?"

DAVID LOOKED AT the receiver in his hand with such a confused expression one would think he'd never seen a telephone before. Hanging up, he called out to Tracker, who was busy in the reception area settling an extremely unsettled Thelma. "Hey, Track? Did you pay your phone bill?"

"Yes," she hollered, annoyed.

"Then why isn't anyone answering at your place?"

David heard running feet; then Tracker was in the side office looking at him accusingly. "What do you mean, no one's answering?"

"I mean no one's answering."

"Are you sure you called the right number?"

David exploded. "Of course I called the right number!" He was about to say a bit more, but there was no point.

Tracker was gone.

THIRTEEN

ALWAYS A LITTLE SLOW on the uptake, when he was on a bender, Freddy was even slower, not realizing for some minutes that the mood of the Indian commercial fisherman had changed from rollicking to downright earnest. By the time he was fully aware of what was being discussed, it came as a jolt that not only were the Indians speaking of a recent murder, but they were also discussing the very woman he was looking for. Chugging down the last of his beer, Freddy leaned over the top of the bar, his befuddled brain doing its best to absorb some of the words his ears were hearing. A few minutes later, having asked a seemingly innocent question, Freddy was smiling like an ugly ape.

HE WAS ONLY slightly drunk now, the night air too crisp to maintain a good binge. Freddy charged for the cover of yet another tree, his breath fogging behind him. Safe behind the base of an impressive red pine, he could taste the threat of snow on his tongue as he licked his lips just before firing off an entire clip, the rounds finding their way through the windows of the darkened cabin. He'd still had most of his beer high when he'd first shot at the silhouette moving in front of the drawn curtains. He'd been drunk enough to feel gleeful when the shadow had fallen. Then, unexpectedly, the cabin had gone dark. He was sober enough to know that the lights should not have gone out—not if she was dead. So, drat, he'd only wounded her. Well, Freddy wasn't one for sloppy kills. He began walking toward the cabin, and with each step he fired off a round just for the hell of it. Something of a "Ding dong, the bitch is gonna be dead" motif.

Freddy's beer sodden jubilation had quickly ended when returning fire came from the cabin.

AN OLD DREAM was suddenly brought to Tracker's mind the instant David had complained about her telephone. The dream, nightmare really, had been about an enormous monster prowling through the woods around her cabin. There had also been something about raspberries, but as she sped along the bone-jarring washboard surface of Blueberry Road, she didn't bother trying to puzzle that last one through. Dream and forebodings aside, she knew for a certainty that there was nothing wrong with her telephone. It was working perfectly and the ringer was set on loud so she would be able to hear it when she was in the workroom at the potter's wheel. Even all the way in the back of the cabin and over the whir of the wheel, she could hear the ring of that phone. When she'd left them, Michael and Benny were in the front room, the phone approximately four feet away. They couldn't possibly not have heard it. They most certainly should have answered. That they hadn't meant trouble.

Big bad monster trouble.

She hadn't loitered in the Courthouse office merely to bother David with yet another of her hunches. On all fronts she was tired of bothering David. Whatever might be going on out on her land assignment, inside her very own house, she'd handle by herself.

THE TRUCK'S WINDOWS were rolled up tight and the noisy heater was going full blast, but she still heard gunfire. The truck's headlights would announce her arrival long before she entered her drive. The only means of extinguishing the Lights on for Safety feature of her practically new Chevy S-10 was to shut down the engine. Doing that left her coasting to the side of the road. She also had to pull the key out so the Key Reminder wouldn't ding dementedly and to punch the dome light button, thus preventing the interior lighting from shining like a beacon in the darkness the instant she opened the door. Once outside the cab, she could hear gunfire even more clearly. Stomach tight, Tracker raced to the rear of the truck, letting down the tailgate. Climbing up and in, she went for the utility box stretching the width of the truck bed and bolted into either side wall. The moon was giving off enough light for an experienced deep woods dweller, but at the moment, because of the truck's dashboard lights, she felt as blind as a newly born bat.

Gunshots sounded again as her hands frantically worked the combination lock on the utility box, ears tuned to the soft clicks. Finally the hasp released and she raised the lid, reaching inside and hurriedly feeling through the box's contents. Her first encounter was with her rolled and tied sleeping bag. She pulled that out, threw it over the side. Next her hands touched the plastic lids of the two large coffee cans containing stuck-in-the-snow survival goodies: instant soups, three candles, and two Sterno cans. The coffee cans quickly went the way of the sleeping bag, the resounding *clunk* each made as they hit the ground almost as loud as the distant gunfire. She didn't have time to worry that the noise might carry as she madly flailed through more of the flotsam cluttering the utility box. She was searching for her dad's thirty-thirty. Then with a groan, she realized she'd given it back. She was about to get back in the truck, highball it for David, when she remembered that there *was* one weapon at the bottom of the box, buried under the debris. After what felt like an eternity, she touched the curve of the Bear-Whitetail compound bow.

The bow had been a birthday gift from her brother Reggie. He was a rabid bow hunter, the only one on Red Cliff. Reggie badly wanted a partner for bow hunting—hence the gift. Trouble was, Tracker didn't care much for bow hunting and as a consequence hadn't replaced the four target arrows in the mounted quiver, Easton XX 75 field tips, with the hunters. The extremely lethal broad-head hunting arrows were at this moment stored safely inside in her gun cabinet. For a heartbeat she felt utterly defeated, was once again ready to make the mad drive back for David.

Then there came another burst of gunfire.

OLD INDIAN Trick Number 37—the hurry-up cure for night blindness. Admittedly this trick plays havoc with one's depth perception, and it's particularly dangerous when applying old Number 37 in a run through a forest. Tracker's one advantage was that this forest was part of her Tribal land assignment and that she knew every tree and stump. Trusting in that knowledge, she kept her right eye tightly closed while making the dash.

The gunfire lessened. Inside a pause, the woods were winter quiet, utterly still. Huffing for breath, clouds of steam billowing from her mouth, she looked like a female Popeye as she armed the bow and waited. Minutes ticked by. The silence of the woods was absolute. And then it was broken by loud and rapid reports, but from a different direction. Either there was more than one shooter, or there was just the one doing a snakelike advance on her cabin.

Tracker was about to bet her very life on the latter.

SHE'D FOUND HIM mostly by following the sounds of his rifle, but as the sight in her left eye improved, she'd been able to place his exact location by watching for the small bursts of light thrown by rifle fire. Judging from the noise and then the subsequent light show, the shooter was using a semiautomatic, most probably a Ruger. Questions as to why someone was shooting at her cabin were brushed aside as she pulled back on the bow, opened her right eye, squinted the left shut.

Trick Number 37 had worked a treat. Through the bow's side-mounted scope she was able with her right eye to see her target. She was gloveless and the bow had a fifty-pound pull. The bowstring bit deep into the tops of her exposed fingers as she strained, brought her thumb to the corner of her mouth. Then, because of modern technology, the pull was suddenly twenty pounds—a weight she could hold without effort for as long as necessary. The shadowy hulk moved little more than a half step to the side. Tracker kept the sight fixed on the center of the huge target, took in a deep breath, held it. The silencers on the hunting bow made the snap of the string sound no louder than a *pfffft*. Tracker wasn't even aware she'd released the arrow until the dark woods were filled with an ungodly howl.

WHEN IT CAME TO the subject of pain, Freddy understood only that he enjoyed giving it. No one had ever truly hurt Freddy before. Yet now pain had suddenly struck him with such force that it turned his bowels into jelly. Stunned, he reached around to the injured area and felt something long, slender, and metal. He didn't feel higher along the rod because he was freaked out by the sticky stuff oozing over his fingertips. In the moonlight the stuff looked black, but Freddy the kneecap breaker knew exactly what it was. It was blood—his blood.

Freddy commenced to howl.

MUSHY WAS FRANTIC. The bedroom door was firmly closed. With each gunshot, Mushy barked and clawed at the door, but the snoring old man on the bed, wrapped like a mummy inside the quilt, refused to wake up. When the howling began, Mushy took a more direct approach, doing the one thing his mistress absolutely did not allow.

Mushy jumped on the bed.

MICHAEL AND BENNY crouched beneath the edge of the blown-out main window. Hearing the unearthly sound, Michael took a chance, raised his head just enough to peer over the window's frame. The bellowing caused the hairs on the back of his neck to stand on end. He quickly slumped down, sitting with his back against the solid log wall. "What the hell is that?"

Benny, sitting shoulder to shoulder beside him, shook his head. "Could be a wolf. Coyote, maybe."

"Which one?"

"Hell if I know. I've never heard a wolf or a coyote sound like that."

Michael fumed with impatience. "Then why did you say a wolf or a coyote?"

"You seem so damned spooked," Benny said dryly, "I wanted to be a comfort."

Before Michael could respond, the ceiling fan lights flared on. The four bulbs emitted enough candlepower to give a mole unerring sight. And there in the center of the blaze stood Tracker's old uncle, clad in yellowish long johns that sagged beneath his skinny butt and tented above his knobbly knees. He was holding Tracker's dog by the collar, the dog twisting and squirming to get free. The old man didn't notice the dog; he was too busy surveying the damaged front room. Then he looked at the huddled pair accusingly. "What the hell you two been doin'?"

"Turn off those lights!" Michael yelled.

With the aid of the bright lights, Tracker's deaf uncle was able to read the younger man's lips perfectly. "I will not," Uncle Bert huffed.

That horrible howl again echoed through the silent woods. The dog rose up on its hind legs and snarled directly into its captor's face. Startled, the old man let go. The next thing Michael and Benny knew, a furred belly was sailing over their heads as the dog leapt through the shattered window. They heard the dog land awkwardly on the front porch, then scramble for purchase, nails digging into the front porch's wooden floorboards. Confused, the old man looked quickly again at the two men huddled just below the window frame.

Michael and Benny hustled to catch him, but the old man was amazingly spry, going for the front door, opening it and rushing out before they had a ghost of a chance at stopping him.

POSSIBLY OLD NUMBER 37 wasn't quite as effective as it should have been, or what was more likely the case, Tracker hadn't gotten around to sighting in the bow. She knew she'd hit the guy because his bulky form had gone down. But as to just where she'd hit him, she couldn't say. What she did know was that he was rolling around and baying horribly and he wouldn't be doing any of that if she'd gotten a clean center back shot. Now her fear was that the Incredible Bulk would still be able to hold and use his

rifle. While fleetingly pondering this, she heard
Mushy; then she saw the form of her dog speeding
straight for the man writhing on the ground. Immediately protective of her mutt, Tracker began to
run.

FREDDY COULDN'T BELIEVE the night he was having—first the unspeakable pain and now a wolf
blasting out of the darkness to finish him off. He
raised an arm just as the wolf came down on top of
him. The wolf's great maw latched on, Freddy able
to feel its sharp teeth sinking all the way through
the insulated sleeve of his subzero weather parka.
The wolf's snarl was horrifying, its breath hot and
foul. Crying like a baby and fighting for his life,
Freddy flailed about with his free hand, frantically
grappling for his rifle.

Tracker beat Uncle Bert to the spot by a mere
second. Doing his best to fight off Mushy, the big
man almost had his hand on the rifle stock. Tracker
immediately kicked the weapon out of his reach,
then picked it up. Recognizing Freddy as the killer
of his dogs, Uncle Bert stood over the downed man
and the battling dog loudly encouraging Mushy to
kill as Tracker hurriedly checked the rounds still remaining in the clip of the Ruger. An instant later
Michael and Benny were also there. She tossed the
Ruger to Benny, then commanded—over her uncle's
voice, the snarls of her dog, and the screams of the

big man—Mushy to release. She yelled "Release!" a second and a third time, but either Mushy was too frenzied to listen or he simply couldn't hear her. Benny tossed the Ruger to Michael, who horrified by the chaotic scene, caught the weapon only as a means of avoiding being hit by it. Benny jumped in to help Tracker pull Mushy off, and after several desperate moments, Mushy fighting against the combined hold on his collar, the dog obeyed. Benny held on to Mushy by wrapping his arms around Mushy's shoulders while Tracker spoke to her dog in clear, no-nonsense tones.

Uncle Bert was kneeling by the man on the ground, yelling at him. "You just keep on twistin' and I'll have the dog on you again. This time I'll let him tear your throat out. It's what you deserve, dog killer."

Whimpering and shaking, Freddy pleaded with the deaf man. "I didn't wanna kill your dogs, Mister. I like dogs. But I was told to do it. They made me. Please, don't let that dog hurt me no more."

"Speak up, son!" Bert hollered.

Exhaling deeply, shaking her head, Tracker touched her uncle's shoulder, gestured for him to move away. Uncle Bert was stubborn, but eventually he complied and she was able to maneuver him back. She whistled for Mushy and the dog slunk forward, sitting down close to Uncle Bert's legs. A modicum of order had been restored. And then Benny started up.

"Ho-le!" Benny cried. He was standing over the man on the ground, clearly able to see the arrow shaft protruding from the big man's posterior. He looked back over his shoulder to Tracker. In a tone loaded with awe, he said, "What a great shot!"

Since childhood, the moments when she'd earned Benny Peliquin's unabashed respect were the most precious to remember. Now was not one of those moments. Unable to meet his eyes, she said softly, "I was aiming for the center of his back."

For a space of seconds everyone was quiet, even the big man. Then Benny burst out laughing and Tracker was instantly sorry she'd told the truth.

"Well, it was dark, ya know?"

Benny doubled over.

Becoming genuinely offended, Tracker hollered, "Shut up, Ben!" But Benny couldn't. Waving his hands he walked in circles and continued laughing like a loon.

Michael came back to his senses. "Does anybody know this guy?"

Uncle Bert hadn't heard Michael, but yelling to his niece, he answered the question nonetheless. "I know who that is! He's the dog killer I was tellin' you about. The one that killed every one of my baby boys." He quickly demanded of Michael, "Son, give me that damn gun."

UNCLE BERT'S FERVID request was denied. In between Freddy's shrieks of "Oh God, somebody help me," and "Don't let that wolf get me!" Tracker left to fetch her truck. Some minutes later, with all four people pulling and straining in an almighty effort, Freddy was loaded into the truck's flatbed. Unable to trust either Uncle Bert or Mushy for more than a second in the presence of the wounded prisoner, she stuck those two in the cab with her, consigning Michael and Benny to the flatbed. Then came the wild ride for the Red Cliff Clinic.

LOOKING BACK over her shoulder, seeing the strobe lights of Bayfield County sheriff's cars across the way in the courthouse lot, Wanda's knees were knocking and her stomach was fluttering with butterflies as she entered the police station. She was expecting to find Ricky chained to something, most probably a radiator, but he wasn't. He was sitting quite comfortably in a chair, thumbing through a magazine. The two cops and the elderly dispatcher were in an opposite corner, seated in a semicircle and talking among themselves in low tones. Everyone looked up as she came in. She sent Ricky a look that conveyed more confidence than she felt, then proceeded on to the half circle of cops.

"Whatever you think he did, he didn't do it. He was with me."

"Huh," Joey Du Bey said. Leaning back in the

chair, he caught and then tried to hold on to Wanda's skittering eyes. It was like trying to catch an eel barehanded. Joey decided simply to stare at the bridge of her nose, allow those flickering eyes to meet his every few seconds.

"Any particular time on this 'with me' alibi, Wanda?" Joey asked sarcastically. "Or is this just a one-lie-fits-all kinda deal?"

Wanda became incensed. "You can believe anything you want, *Officer Du Bey*." She made his rank and name sound like an incurable disease. "I've called an attorney in Bayfield. He'll be here in an hour."

"Cool," Joey replied. He nodded toward Doc Ricky. "Then just go park your butt over there with your boyfriend, and we'll all wait."

As DOC RICKY WAS unavailable, there was no one qualified to give emergency care. Then, too, there was a problem the night nurse pointed out over the wounded man's highly vocal pleas.

The patient lay belly-down on the gurney, a man so huge that his long legs hung over the end, the toes of his boots scraping flooring. The four wielding the gurney had burst in through the back bay doors, an entrance to be used by medical personnel only. Improper use of the staff door infuriated the pure starch out of Sharon Bear, R.N.

"He's not a tribal member," she said without a

trace of compassion. "So even if I was qualified to treat him, which I'm *not,* I still wouldn't be allowed to touch him."

"Hey!" Michael yelped. "Bayfield County will cover the tab. Just pull the arrow out, slap a Band-Aid on his ass, and send the sheriff's office the bill."

Sharon Bear's temper swelled. Arms tightly folded beneath her ample bosom, she coldly eyed Michael. "I'm afraid it isn't that simple," she replied. "God only knows where that arrow has been, so there's the high risk of infection. Plus, he could be bleeding internally, which means he'll need more attention than we, especially at this hour, are able to give. But"—she sighed heavily as if doing her best to yield to unseemly pressure—"what I could do is call the ambulance to transport him to Ashland."

"Hey," Michael said, openly snide, "could ya? Man, that'd be so nice."

"Drugs!" Freddy screamed. "For the love of God, somebody give me some drugs!"

Tracker bent forward, speaking close to his ear. "Has anyone ever told you that Indians...barter?"

Pushing himself up slightly, bracing his upper torso on his forearms, Freddy stared at her, mouth agape, eyes vacant. "What does that mean?"

"It means if you're a good boy, I'll make sure you get whatever you need to make the pain go away."

FOURTEEN

NURSE SHARON BEAR was a formidable woman, but she'd just met her match in Tracker. Ignoring the woman's carping about a pay telephone being available at the end of the hall, Tracker plugged a finger into the ear Nurse Sharon spoke stridently against while helping herself to the telephone in the nurses' station. The second Elliott Raven came on the other end of the line, Tracker began to yell over the huffy woman's robust complaints.

"I have to talk to David. Now."

"But he's over at the—"

Tracker leapt in. "I said *now*, Elliott. This is an emergency."

"Oh no," the dispatcher breathed heavily. "Not another one." Then hurriedly, "Hang on, girl. I'll have to run over an' get him."

"No," she cried. Finger still stuck in one ear, receiver against the other, she turned at the waist, gave the nurse a baleful glare. Nurse Sharon wasn't bothered. She shifted grievances, began to harp on the subject of the major disruption Tracker and friends were causing her shift. Tracker went back to Elliott.

"Just tell David to get Doc Ricky to the clinic. And tell him to bring handcuffs. Big ones."

Tracker hung up, turned again to Nurse Sharon, a satisfied expression on her face. "The doctor is on his way. And we"—she waved a hand, indicating herself and motley companions—"aren't going anywhere."

Stricken, the nurse looked at the four men—three standing, one draping the gurney with an object protruding from his buttock—as if seeing them for the first time. Benny Peliquin, whom she vaguely knew, and the blond man, whom she didn't know at all, were disheveled and appeared exhausted, as if they'd just come through a war. The old man, clad only in a parka, untied lacrosse snow boots, and foul-looking long johns, was a legend.

Old Bert came to the clinic only when absolutely necessary, and on each occasion raised a whoop and a holler during every minute of his presence. Which meant he was seen by a doctor as rapidly as possible, even if doing so meant the staff jumping him to the front of a lengthy queue. If that old man created one of his infamous ruckuses, he'd wake up the small hospital's few sleeping patients and Nurse Sharon could then effectively kiss goodbye what was normally the easiest shift of the daily schedule. Then there was the matter of the giant on the gurney.

The last thing she needed out of him was one more groan. Pushing the sleeves of her lab coat back to her elbows, Nurse Sharon took charge.

"I'm going to administer a mild sedative to the patient. The rest of you can help yourselves to coffee and take seats in the waiting area."

The nurse moved briskly off, making her way to the med's room. Michael and Benny went for the coffeepot behind the nurse's station. Uncle Bert, looking mildly baffled, followed. Before Tracker could move away, the big man, who was weeping softly, reached out a huge paw. Tracker looked down at the hand fully encircling her lower arm. His hold on her was tight but gentle. She glanced from the hand to the blue-green eyes, eyes that held the fear-crazed look of a wounded animal.

"Please, don't leave Freddy." He sounded like a pleading child.

Although she had more than enough reason to hate this man, Tracker felt moved to pity. "I won't," she said softly, patting the big hand.

Nurse Sharon returned rapidly. Her manner still as frosty as a north wind in January, she held out a tiny paper cup with a single pill inside it. To wash it down, she also offered a splash of water in a second paper cup. The hand on Tracker's arm tightened.

Tracker pushed her face close to the big man's,

speaking sternly. "Take it. It will help against the pain."

The nurse's spine stiffened. "We prefer *discomfort*."

Tracker had had enough of Nurse Sharon's attitude. Her arm was still captured inside the huge hand as she turned away from the gurney and faced down Nurse Sharon. She thoroughly startled the woman when she went on the attack. "Have you ever had an arrow in your ass?"

The nurse blanched, eyebrows shooting to her scalp.

"Obviously not," Tracker continued. "Otherwise you'd know there's a hell of a lot more *pain* than discomfort involved." She turned back to the big man. "Take the damn pill, Freddy, before the nice nurse decides to swallow it herself."

FIVE MINUTES LATER, the pill was taking effect. Freddy was becoming groggy but was still relatively coherent when David, Joey Du Bey, and Doc Ricky came breezing in. Freddy's droopy eyes locked on the latter.

"Hey, Doc," Freddy tipsily hailed. "How's it hangin'?"

Doc Ricky skidded to a halt. Wanda, Doc Ricky's assistant, came charging in. She stopped short, barely avoiding a collision with the doctor's back.

She stepped around him; then, seeing the man on the gurney, Wanda went pale, clutched Doc Ricky's arm.

Tracker squirmed out of the big man's hold, went to stand between Joey and David. Joey placed a light hand against the small of her back, sending her a hope-filled smile when she glanced up at him. She looked away, her eyes on David's broad back as David took in Doc Ricky's and Wanda's instant reactions to the enormous patient with an arrow in his rear end. And on that subject, a bewildered David turned to Tracker. "Where the hell did the arrow come from?"

Tracker rolled her eyes toward the ceiling and lifted her hands, shrugging.

"Did you do that?" he asked, astounded.

Tracker sent him a sideways glance. "Maybe."

David puffed up like a bullfrog. "Oh, for Christ's sake, Track!"

Doc Ricky, with Nurse Sharon hovering at his elbow, was examining the patient. "I've got to get him into surgery." He glanced across to his assistant. "Wanda, you're scrubbing with me." Then to the nurse by his side: "Take him behind the exam curtain and get him prepped. Have him ready for showtime in ten minutes."

Blearily, Freddy followed the conversation. As the doctor sped off and Nurse Sharon and an orderly began rolling the gurney, Freddy let out a whispery whistle, signaling for Tracker. As she joined them, trotting alongside the moving gurney, the big man sought her hand, grabbed onto it like a lifeline.

"I'm afraid of that woman," he slurred.

The gurney, considering that it was overloaded and propelled only by an orderly and one nurse, was picking up an impressive speed. During the jog, Tracker peered back over her shoulder at Nurse Sharon.

FREDDY DIDN'T SEEM all that afraid anymore as the nurse and orderly cut away his clothing, bathed him in alcohol from his shoulders down to his knees, then applied a liquid that stained his big buttock puke-yellow. Tracker did her best not to watch any of the prepping procedure as she held the man's hand.

"You know," she said, "when I was a little girl, I wanted to be a nun."

"Huh." Freddy wasn't interested.

Tracker continued regardless. "I used to practice keeping secrets. You know, preparing myself for when I had to hear confessions."

Freddy rolled a glassy eye, tried to make it focus on her. He licked dry lips, his tongue thick from the sedative. "Nuns can do that kinda stuff too, eh?"

"Sure they can," Tracker said. "But only in emergencies. When a life is threatened. Like now."

Freddy squinted up at her. "Somebody gonna die?"

"Yes. You might."

Freddy became agitated. "Me?"

He was squeezing her hand so tightly, Tracker worried about her fingers. She pried at his hand as she continued. "Now, Freddy, I know you don't want them to put you to sleep while you're in trouble with God. I think you ought to talk to me."

Freddy mulled, looked at her again. "Then me an' God? We'd be okey-doke?"

"Yes."

"Even if I've been real, real bad?"

"Yes."

Freddy labored over that one, then erupted. "Hey! You're not a nun! You can't fix shit." He nodded his head as his eyes hardened. "An' I'm startin' to think it was you that shot me."

Tracker freed her hand. "All right, then, I'll get someone else to hear your confession."

Smug now, Freddy answered with a snort. "Good. 'Cause I just remembered, Freddy don't like you."

SHE FOUND David and Joey in the scrub room, both dressed in green cotton scrubs, paper shower caps on their heads, paper booties on their feet, and disposable masks hanging around their necks by an elastic band.

"Rick's still our prime suspect for absolutely everything," David explained. "We have to go in and watch him operate. Make certain he doesn't get hinkey with a witness that has more courtroom potential than your uncle Bert.''

''Great,'' Tracker said irritably. ''But before they put your witness out like a light, you ought to talk to him. And put that mask on so he can't see your face.'' She grabbed his arm to encourage him along.

''Hey! You're not allowed to touch me.''

Tracker didn't care. She pulled him along regardless and murmured under her breath, too low for him to hear, ''Oh, if you'd only thought to say that to Sharrie.''

THE OPERATION WENT quickly, Doc Ricky cussing all through it, saying more than once, ''If this had been a hunting arrow, this guy would have bled out.''

The procedure was witnessed by David, and technically by Joey. Although Joey had been physically present, during the first incision, Joey had fainted. David didn't catch him, merely watched, thoroughly amused, as Joey fell over like a tree. Once the patient was in the small hospital's lone recovery room, David, still in scrubs, had a quiet word with Michael and Benny, giving Michael the keys to Tracker's truck.

Head down, Benny kept his hands shoved deep inside his pockets as he listened. Michael worked the keys in his hand as he too listened, his expression incredulous. "You can't mean it," he said after David finished.

David didn't have time to go through it all again. "Look, that's what the man said. And his statement was witnessed by me, Tracker, a nurse, and an orderly."

Michael still wasn't buying any of it. "But he was medicated, right? That means it's not admissible. Not even if you brought God into the courtroom as a witness."

David wanted to hit something. The Bayfield deputy was looking a bit too handy. "Just go to the P.D. and wait. I'll be there just as soon as I can."

"Shouldn't we all go together?" Michael wanted to know.

"We could, but that nurse won't let me leave until I've had a shower."

Benny looked askance. "Why?"

David threw his arms wide. "Beats the snot out of me. All I know is, she won't give me my damn clothes until she's sure I've scrubbed everything. Including Mister Peepee."

Benny's eyebrows lifted. "Whoa, Mister Peepee. Now that's some serious showerin'. She gonna be givin' you a pecker check to make sure you did everything right?"

David was appalled. For several seconds he gaped at Benny, utterly speechless. Then his face scrunched into a severe frown. "That's a real killer. Ben." David turned to Michael. "Track's dog is still in her truck. He'll act like he wants to eat your ass when you get near the truck. He always does that and Tracker thinks that's just so wonderful. What she doesn't know is, her dog has a weak spot. And if you swear not to tell, I'll let you in on the secret."

"Hey," Michael said, "I saw the way that thing went after Goliath. I'm not interested in having it do that to me."

David stepped closer, speaking conspiratorially. "Okay, here's what you say…"

In the hospital parking lot, Benny and a bemused Michael stood near Tracker's S-10. Behind the rolled-up window, Mushy was a mass of happy wiggles.

"Well, I'll be damned." Michael was amazed. He glanced at Benny. "Say it again."

Benny complied. "Hey, ugly! Wanna go for jerky?"

Mushy whined louder, scratched at the glass barrier.

"Be damned!" Michael exclaimed. "So now what do we do?"

"We get in the truck and take his squirmy ass to Buffalo Bay Store for some jerky."

TRACKER WAS WONDERING where David had gotten to as she sat with Joey in the corner of the waiting area. Joey had been remarkably shaken by the brief stint in the operating room.

"Man," he rambled, "it was gross. Had to be the biggest ass I ever seen. Then Doc Ricky started cutting into it." Joey shuddered, his eyes sliding sideways to meet Tracker's. Then Joey's eyes lit up as his tone became electrified. "There was all this yellow gunk. Looked like fuckin' chicken fat!" Joey began shaking his head. "I don't remember anything after that." He looked at Tracker again, his manly pride in dire need of empathy. "It was the ether fumes. They really knocked me out, ya know?"

Tracker was rubbing Joey's hand, giving him the *there, there* treatment as Nurse Sharon marched toward them. Having shared the experience of pre-op confessor, Nurse Sharon wasn't feeling especially steady, either, but the woman was still in charge of the night shift, thus required to remain scrupulous to duty. And with Joey Du Bey at any rate, she seemed much more agreeable with the idea of being a compassionate nurse.

"I'm taking him to the break room for a cup of coffee," she informed Tracker. "Then I have to make certain he showers."

Apparently these decisions were set in stone. Nurse Sharon helped Joey to his feet, slung an arm around his scrub-clothed waist and held his hand as she led him off. Tracker was left to stare at their backs until they disappeared. The emergency room had become as still as a stagnant pond. Other than the beige walls, there was nothing for her to watch or even read. One boring minute after another crawled by. Finally, carrying his beloved baseball cap in his hand and dressed in a flannel shirt, jeans, his boots and a light jacket, David came striding into the open waiting area. His long hair, pulled back in a ponytail, looked wet. He stopped in front of her and slammed the cap down on his head.

While he was adjusting the cap he issued orders. "You're coming with me," he said. "You and I are escorting the doc and Wanda back to the station."

Tracker stood up from the hard plastic chair. "What about my uncle?"

David puffed air through his lips. "Ah, hell, he's asleep in one of the exam rooms. When we get back to the station, I'll have Elliott call your dad to come get him."

"But Uncle Bert's a witness," she insisted. "He should come to the station, too."

David's patience was tapped dry. "Look," he said sharply, "it's a small station, okay? And God knows once we get there, the place is gonna fill up fast."

EVEN AS DAVID SPOKE the Red Cliff Police Department was already standing room only. The Tribal Chairman and the Bayfield County Sheriff were in the midst of a heated argument with Elliott Raven.

The cause of the argument, Benny, stood with his hands cuffed behind him and in between two Bayfield deputies. Elliott was trying in vain to bring a smidgen of order to the situation, and Mel, head going back and forth between the chairman and the sheriff, sat slack-jawed on top of a desk.

A highly frustrated Michael wiped his face with his hands. Sheriff Bothwell wasn't interested in anything Michael had to say. Despite Michael's repeated assurances that Benny couldn't have possibly killed the BIA agent, Bothwell was satisfied he had the right man. Benny Peliquin was a serial killer. That was that, case closed.

Meanwhile, huddled in the farthest corner, Thelma Frenchette looked tiny in her chair. Her head bowed, arms on thighs, fingers entwined around a Styrofoam cup, she stared bleakly into a cup of coffee. She looked up as David ushered Ricky and Wanda into the station. Behind them came Tracker. Seeing her, Thelma's eyes livened a bit, then, noticing the file Tracker carried in one arm, Thelma's eyes went dull again.

The station was crowded and Tracker less than a couple of feet away, but because of the deputies containing Benny, she couldn't maneuver any closer to Thelma. She had to stand to the side, watching the older woman slide further into despondency. And Tracker understood the cause of her despair. In relinquishing the file, Thelma had failed Perry Frenchette. Failing Perry meant that Thelma's days as an exemplary member of the prestigious Frenchette clan were finished. Looking as if she wished she could just simply disappear, Thelma again gazed wearily into the cup of coffee.

David had walked headlong into the fierce argument, putting himself between his dispatcher, the chairman, and the sheriff. Elliott was noticeably relieved as the chairman and the sheriff, glaring at David, stepped back.

To the two deputies, David barked, "Take those damn cuffs off that man."

Other than to shift their eyes toward Bothwell, neither deputy moved. The sheriff spoke for them. "Benny Peliquin is now in my custody, under arrest for the double homicide."

David exploded. "That's bullshit and you know it!"

Bothwell assumed a pained but calmer aspect. Fixing his attention on David, the sheriff proceeded. "This reservation is under my jurisdiction, and until I'm overturned in a court of law, what I decide is final."

Using his first two fingers, David beckoned Tracker. Wedging herself through the bodies, she hastened forward. David ripped the file out of her arms, held it up, waved it in Bothwell's round face. "I've just upped the ante."

"What the hell is that?" Bothwell demanded.

David breathed steam through his nose. "Let's just call it a list."

Bothwell treated David to one of his hearty laughs, then cried, "Well, whoop-de-doo. The boy's got a list!"

"Yeah," David said. "And your name's on it."

Bothwell stopped laughing.

David stepped up to the sheriff, spoke as professionally as his simmering anger would allow. "You are under arrest for the willful destruction of federally protected land."

The sheriff whirled away, yelling, "Damn you, Frenchette!"

Watching her illustrious in-law wilt before her very eyes caused Thelma to perk up. She knocked back the tepid coffee, set the Styrofoam cup down by her feet. Then she sat up in the chair, spine rigidly straight, hands folded in her lap, eyes bright and alert. Something terrible was about to happen to Perry. Considering the terrible way he had tried to use her, to involve her in whatever he was up to, then had spoken so callously to her and had made threats against her future as a tribal employee, Thelma'd be damned before she missed one second of his ruin.

MICHAEL, NOW SITTING on top of the desk alongside his new best pal Benny, looked as happy as a kid on Christmas morning. On the other side of Benny was Tracker. David, standing in the center of the squad room, was holding forth as Mel, a rifle held across his chest, stood guard over the seated sheriff and Tribal Chairman. Directly behind the desk, and seated next to Thelma Frenchette, were the two now thoroughly flustered Bayfield County deputies. The only thing keeping them in the chairs was Michael's assurance that he would take any and all heat this little wander down the Yellow Brick Road might engender. And as he was somehow related to the lieutenant governor...

TRACKER WAS ANTSY, squirming around. Michael leaned forward, looking around Benny. He didn't know her all that well, but he'd learned enough in the last hours to know when she was fuming. He reached across, touched her leg. Gaining her attention, he mouthed, "What's wrong?"

Frowning with all her might, she stabbed her index finger in the air, as if her finger were a knife pointing at David. Michael's blond head snapped back, eyes widening in surprise.

"He's getting everything backward!" she urgently whispered.

David heard her. As did Bothwell, who turned enough of his bulk to look at her over his shoulder. With a forced laugh the sheriff said, "You tell him, gal!"

Tracker's eyes met David's. She couldn't ever recall seeing him so angry, his expression so...cold. David turned at the waist and let the file fall from his hand. It landed on the nearest desktop with a thump. "Yeah," he said, tone wintry, "why don't you just stand up and point out where I've gone wrong." His icy black eyes touched hers again. "It's what you do best."

FIFTEEN

DAVID, BOILING WITH RAGE, had issued a challenge. And to make sure she accepted, had thrown in the barb. The small squad room was thick with tension, all eyes on her as she slid off the desk.

"I only meant to point out," she said, hating the shake in her voice, "that you're putting the murders ahead of everything."

David sneered. "Oh, pardon me for thinking the deaths of two men are important."

"Well, of course they are," she snapped. "But why they were killed is even more important."

Her voice wasn't shaking now. Everyone, with the exception of David, had ceased to exist. Tracker spoke only to him.

"It was easy to blame Benny for Jud because Thelma"—Tracker waved an arm in Thelma's direction—"said Benny was the last one to see him. That they were having a loud argument when she left." She turned to Thelma, and Thelma nodded rapidly.

"That's right," Thelma hurriedly supplied. "I heard them all over the building."

"When you were turning off lights and making certain the building was secure."

"Yes. I do that every evening before I leave."

"So," Tracker encouraged, "to your knowledge, other than yourself, Jud, and Benny, there was no one else in the building."

Thelma sat ramrod straight, head high. "There was no one else," she declared. "I absolutely know that for a fact."

"What about the parking lot?" Tracker pressed.

Thelma was thrown by the question. She floundered for a moment, a hand going to her lips. Hesitantly she ventured, "I—I..." Her eyes popped wide. "Wait! There was a car in the lot. I remember wondering..." She looked at Doc Ricky, and in a whisper, finished, ". . . who was sick."

Ricky shook his head while smiling an odd smile. Wanda clutched his arm, hung on tight, tried to gain his attention. Ricky wouldn't look at her.

"Man! The medical examiner did it," Mel exclaimed. "Talk about a killer returning to the scene of the crime!"

Elliott exploded. "Shut up, Mel."

But David was looking hard at Doc Ricky, remembering his excessive nervousness while on the scene. His anger when Michael insisted the body be transported to Ashland for autopsy. The autopsy report wouldn't be ready for another two or three days. Plenty of time for Ricky to head out. The very thing Joey had said it looked to him that the doctor was in the middle of planning when he and Mel picked him up for friendly questioning on the matter of his being seen on the recovery barge.

David's mind went back to the recent confession of the huge man Tracker had brought down with an arrow. He mused aloud, "So, Rick…you're the big boss, eh?"

"No," Tracker interjected, "he's not."

David shot back furiously: "Aw, come on, Track. We've got him cold." He began ticking off the facts on his fingertips. "His car was seen in the courthouse lot. He was seen on the barge. He—"

"…didn't do it," Doc Ricky finished. Having gained their full attention, Ricky stretched out his long legs, did everything but yawn in their collective faces. "I have more than enough witnesses to vouch for the fact that I was at the hospital all that night. Hell, I was still with patients when I got the call to come to the courthouse."

David was livid. "Maybe you have witnesses for murder number one, but what have you got for murder number two?"

"Same-o, same-o." Ricky was arrogant.

David wasn't persuaded. "Then how do you explain Thelma's seeing your car?"

Pursing his lips, Ricky shrugged. "Can't."

"You have the only set of keys?"

"Yes."

"You give them to anybody?"

"No."

Exasperated, Tracker interrupted the sideshow. "He didn't have to give anyone the keys." Heads turned to her. More than a little tempted to thump David, she cried, "You're not thinking again. You're not asking yourself who on Red Cliff has a key to *everyone's* truck or car."

David looked as if he'd just been slapped. Ricky broke out laughing. Wanda DuPree began to sob. Michael jumped off the desk, and beginning with Bothwell, began arresting damn near everybody.

THEY LEANED AGAINST her truck, watching cars pull out, bubble lights throbbing, sirens whooping, all of the occupants in the cars headed for Bayfield County jail and bologna sandwich suppers.

"Another thing you forgot," Tracker said, exhaling cigarette smoke, "is that Arrow Man—"

"I still can't believe you shot him with an arrow!" David yelped. He flipped his cigarette away, the glowing red dot sailing into the area of the parking lot the milk-white glow of the single halogen light didn't reach. David pushed himself off the truck, stood facing her. "Don't you think that was just a little *too* Indianish?"

"I didn't have anything else."

David grunted. "I'm still not buying it."

Tracker waved an angry hand, took another lungful of nicotine. "Oh, who the hell cares. Are you going to listen or not?"

Defeated, David shoved his hands in his jeans pockets. "I'm listening."

Satisfied, Tracker continued. "Okay, maybe it slipped past you, but Arrow Man doesn't exactly click on all six cylinders. The clue to that one is his reference to himself in the third person. 'Freddy wants this,'" she mimicked. "'Freddy's afraid.'" She inhaled again, then tossed her cigarette in the same direction David had. "He got my attention when he said Freddy was afraid of that woman. At the time I thought he meant the nurse, but then I noticed that he wasn't acting afraid when she was present. In fact when he got mad at me, he seemed more than glad to be left alone with the nurse while I went off to look for you. But he was still fearful, enough to confess all his sins to Father David. And why?" she asked rhetorically. "Because the woman he was afraid of would be with him in the operating room. In other words, Wanda."

"How did he know to be afraid of her?"

"Killer recognition, David. It's as simple as that. Good ole Freddy had to have known Wanda. She barely allowed Ricky out of her sight. So the day Uncle Bert spotted him on the barge, you can bet your gums Wanda was there, too. But probably in the wheelhouse, which would explain why my uncle didn't see her."

David knuckled his eyes. "Okay, she confessed to both murders and now she's clammed up until she can get a lawyer, but I still don't know why she'd kill Jud or the Navajo."

"She did it for Ricky," Tracker said flatly.

"He told her to?"

"No, she killed Jud because he was becoming a loose cannon, the talk of the rez. Ricky must have worried out loud that if you took Jud in for knocking around Imogen and he'd been drinking, well, that he might say a little too much on the subject of trees."

"So she shoots Jud just to ease Ricky's worried mind?"

Tracker let go a sour laugh. "You'd be amazed what a woman will do for her man." She quickly changed the subject. "But Wanda wasn't totally ir-rational. She used effort in distancing herself from the murders. She lifted Ricky's keys from her hus-band's master set so she could leave her car in the hospital's lot for all to see while Ricky's was on the scene. The gun most probably belongs to her hus-band. That way, should things turn sour, she can point in two different directions and cry, 'They did it!' And if she's as smart as I believe she is, that's exactly what she'll still do. Of course, she'll still have to contend with me. If you'll recall, I followed her footprints around the building and then found the same print in the office in the Navajo's blood.'' Tracker looked smug. ''I'll make a great witness. I think I'll wear my blue skirt to the trial.''

''What do you think she did with Jud's original file?''

''Oh, I don't think she ever saw it. I think the file we found is the original.'' She smiled slyly. ''If you wanted to hide something, where better than Hildy's files?''

David tossed back his head, smiling to the heavens. ''Hell, you could lose anything in there.''

''Exactly. But after the many searches everyone did in Jud's office, it occurred to Perry where it most likely had to be. So he sent Thelma in. Just one more woman doing for the man she adores.''

David looked at her, smiling that heart-melting smile of his. ''I was just wondering. Does shooting a Chamook in the butt with an arrow qualify as something a woman would do for the man she adored?''

Tracker's face puckered. ''Put a sock in it, David.''

''Hey, I was just asking.'' He turned and leaned against the truck, settling close to her.

They looked up at the stars for several moments. The night was clear, the air sharp. Tracker accepted his warmth without complaint. ''Arrow Man of course meant Bothwell,'' she said tiredly, ''when he talked about the big boss. Big, in Arrow Man's mind, meaning fat. And when you think about it, who else has the connections? Or knows the area and the day-to-day habits of Red Cliffers better? He needed Jud to do the contracting, Frenchette to wangle the nearby legal clear-cutting operation so that the equipment would be in place, and the Navajo to keep the BIA at arm's length.''

"So where did Ricky fit?''

"That's something only Ricky can tell us. If he ever will,'' she amended. "But my best guess is that he simply caught on and went after the money.''

"Blackmail, eh?''

"Sort of. But with Ricky''—she shook her head—"my gut says he wanted the money for altruistic reasons.''

David looked speculatively at her. "You know, now that you mention it, he was getting a lot of big budget approvals. I bitched about Frenchette laying new carpet all over everything, but the truth is, I was more resentful that all Ricky had to do was ask for any new thing he wanted, while I couldn't even get my department a decent coffeepot.''

"Well,'' Tracker sighed, moving away from him, "there you go then. The mystery of our tribal budget is finally solved.'' Stretching her arms over her head, she yawned, "I'm pooped.'' Arms settling at her sides, she said, "I'm ready to go home and have a nice hot bath.''

David took the hint. Pushing away from the truck, he began walking away. "Enjoy it, babe. You earned it."

"And don't forget the two hundred dollars in tracking fees," she yelled at his back.

Laughing, David kept walking.

ELLIOTT WAS LEAVING, packing it in for the day. "Hey," he said as David walked through the door. "That Bjorke guy wants you to call him. He sounds upset again."

"Ah, God," David groaned. "What now?"

"Jailbreak maybe. Tell me in the morning." Elliott was gone, the door swinging shut behind him.

David went to a desk, punched the speed-dial button for Bayfield county sheriff. Michael answered, sounding hysterical. "You are just never going to believe this."

"What?"

"I'm the new sheriff!"

David grinned. "Excuse me? How did you get elected so fast?"

"I'm appointed," Michael fumed, "by my own asshole uncle. Did I forget to tell you he's the lieutenant governor?"

"Yeah, you did kinda forget that one."

Michael didn't care. "Well, he is. And as Bothie still owes two years in term, I'm stuck serving them out."

"Hey, congratulations!" David laughed.

"Suck salt and die, Lameraux." Michael slammed the phone down.

Staring at the receiver in his hand, David continued laughing.

AT TWELVE P.M. on the next day, Imogen was a hollow shell of herself as she came off the plane, walking unsteadily beside her father. She was fully expecting every law officer in the state of Wisconsin to meet her at the end of the tunnel. What she did not expect was Benny, standing there with a bouquet of flowers. And with a cry she ran to him, flinging herself into his arms.

"Welcome home, honey," Benny said against her neck.

SHE'D SPENT the entire morning cleaning her cabin, trying to put right the things that last night's shootout had damaged. Her father and brothers would be coming soon to repair her windows. Dressed in a sweat shirt and jeans, Tracker enjoyed the calm before the family storm descended. She was taking a break, sitting on the top stair of the front porch steps sipping coffee and stroking Mushy's shaggy fur. A minute before she'd heard a hunting eagle's scream. Now she was listening to the woodpeckers tapping at bugs high up in the trees. With the warmth of the sun on her face, Tracker breathed contentedly.

Just another day in North Woods paradise.

DESPERATE JOURNEYS

Four trips you *won't* want to take…

DESERT DECEIT by Betty Webb
The murder of a media magnate turns a dude-ranch cattle drive into a trail full of unforeseen danger. Vacationing private eye Lena Jones attempts to unmask a killer in Arizona's most rugged and remote area.

THE FIRST PROOF by Terence Faherty
Ex-seminarian Owen Keane accompanies his former lover to Maine to bury her estranged husband. But dark mysteries surrounding the dead man's family converge as a murderer strikes at the heart of a tragic past filled with buried secrets, blackmail and vengeance.

DEATH ON THE SOUTHWEST CHIEF by Jonathan Harrington
Danny O'Flaherty escorts his eccentric aunt on a cross-country train trip, only to discover his uncle's corpse in the next seat. When the body is stolen and replaced with that of a freshly strangled man, Danny has seventy-two hours to find a killer.

STAR SEARCH by Nancy Baker Jacobs
Hollywood Star reporter Quinn Collins inherits a house from a writer she never knew. Looking into blacklisted writers of the 1950s proves dangerous as Quinn exposes a killer's desperate scheme—and the stunning truth about her own parents.

Available May 2004 at your favorite retail outlet.

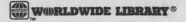

MYSTERY **WORLDWIDE LIBRARY** ®
TM

WDJ491

ED GORMAN
EVERYBODY'S SOMEBODY'S FOOL

A SAM McCAIN MYSTERY

When local bad boy David Egan is accused of murder, lawyer Sam McCain finds himself saddled with a new client...and another tale of small-town murder in Black River Falls, Iowa.

But McCain's client dies a fiery death in a car accident—an event that becomes murder when it's discovered the car's brake lines were cut. Working to clear Egan's name, McCain follows a trail of shattered dreams, cheating spouses, dark secrets to a body lying lifeless in a bath and to a tale of murder that embraces the vast human emotions that drive lovers to love...and killers to kill.

"...a fascinating time machine, recalling the arcana of a more innocent time.'
—*Publishers Weekly*

Available June 2004 at your favorite retail outlet.

 **WORLDWIDE LIBRARY®**

WEG494

THE
DEVIL'S HEARTH
PHILLIP DEPOY

A FEVER DEVLIN MYSTERY

Fever Devlin returns to his
home in the Appalachians,
prepared to confront the
ghosts of his past, but never
expecting to find instead
the corpse of a half brother
he never knew existed.

As he sorts through his quirky
family history, Fever begins to
uncover the festering secrets of
this mountain community where
the dead tell no tales—and a
killer plots to ensure Fever joins
their eternal silence.

"Phillip DePoy is a born
storyteller. To read
The Devil's Hearth is to be
inside an Appalachian
folktale as it unfolds…"
—S. J. Rozan,
winner of the 2003 Edgar
and the 2002 Shamus Awards
for Best Novel.

*Available May 2004 at your
favorite retail outlet.*

WORLDWIDE LIBRARY ®

WPD492